FERAL EYE OF THE BLACKBIRD

FERAL EYE OF THE BLACKBIRD

A Journey Reveals the Power of Reason

A Novel

John Katsoulis

SUNSTONE
PRESS

SANTA FE

Sunstone books may be purchased for educational, business, or sales promotional use.
For information please write: Special Markets Department, Sunstone Press,
P.O. Box 2321, Santa Fe, New Mexico 87504-2321.

Design › R. Ahl
Printed on acid-free paper
∞
eBook 978-1-61139-636-2

Library of Congress Cataloging-in-Publication Data

Names: Katsoulis, John, 1969- author.
Title: Feral eye of the blackbird : a man on a journey discovers the power
    of reason / a novel by John Katsoulis.
Description: Santa Fe, NM : Sunstone Press, 2021. | Includes reader's
    guide. | Summary: "Two white men are kidnapped, sent to an African
    diamond mine as slaves, and must find a way out"-- Provided by
    publisher.
Identifiers: LCCN 2021039699 | ISBN 9781632933546 (paperback) | ISBN
    9781611396362 (epub) | ISBN 1632933543 (paperback)
Subjects: LCGFT: Novels.
Classification: LCC PS3611.A78858 F47 2021 | DDC 813/.6--dc23
LC record available at https://lccn.loc.gov/2021039699

WWW.SUNSTONEPRESS.COM
SUNSTONE PRESS / POST OFFICE BOX 2321 / SANTA FE, NM 87504-2321 /USA
(505) 988-4418

This book is dedicated to my father George Katsoulis, the best man I ever met. He taught me to believe what I see, not see what I believe.

1

Dad always said, "Son, it's a complicated world, and here's my advice: Be careful where you put certain things, and your John Hancock, and you'll be fine." It's made me a certain way, and according to some, maybe too cynical at times. I don't mind it, though, if you knew where I came from, it's considered a badge of honor. But when the company's driver made us sign our Death Benefits Form in the back of the car, I knew we were screwed.

He was driving us to an airport outside New Hope, Pennsylvania, where we were about to fly off to Peru to become rich. Logos, my boss, didn't like him, and neither did I. Let's say, we got a bad feeling about him, and where we were going, and who was behind it, like smelling the air and knowing the rain's coming. Especially when the prick pulled the old Lincoln around a hedge, threw his chin at the door, and told us to get out. He flicked us off and burned rubber away.

We walked toward the tarmac, where an old bird sat. A cargo plane held together by tape, idled with the props turned off. Even the last digits of the registration number peeled off the tail like an old scab. We could've been in the middle of a farm, or national park, or the wastelands of the apocalypse, as there was nothing around, not even a tower. The pneumatic cargo door sank down and so did my stomach. I told myself, keep it together, these people who sent us know what they're doing, and I trusted Logos as much as my dad.

We moved inside and it got dark. Three huge crates took up the fuselage. They smelled like new pine, with *8' x 8'* spray-painted like a gang tag on all sides. I breathed harder, and all the talk I made up back at his office about adventure, the unknown, and making history, got real.

A door opened, and the pilot man came out. The props whirled on, and it got loud as all hell.

"You guys my cargo?" the pilot shouted.

Logos stared at him. *"Where's this plane headed?"*

The pilot pointed to his headset. *"The mine."* He entered the cockpit.

When the cargo door crept up, we looked at each other, not sure what to do. The plane jolted us when it rolled.

"Lean on the wall," Logos said. "We'll get answers."

The plane sped up, men grabbed us, and hoods went over our heads. The last thing I remembered was the smell of acetone.

§

Logos kicked me awake. He grunted through a dirty shirt pulled across his mouth and neck. His eyes pointed down for me to look. We were chained like animals, hands together, feet together, a ton of cloth taped in our mouths. We weren't injured, or anything, but not ourselves anymore either. Without the will of movement, we were less than before, scared half-men, our pasts and wills wiped away clean. My knees shook.

The fear seeped in, slo-mo at first. It seemed like it was happening to someone else, from somewhere else, and we were watching two other guys from the other side of the plane—but no, we were the men in chains.

It hit me, and I was falling and falling, and it felt like falling into ice water, or from a tall building, or I don't know what. Everything compressed, my lungs, my throat, my chest, the size of the plane, and the space see-sawed. If I wasn't sitting down, I would've fallen down. An animal in me groaned, caterwauled, and I hyperventilated, and cried for mommy. My life was over or coming to an end in the next few hours. I was away from everyone I ever knew or loved. Logos's life was over, too. It happened in a blink, like slipping off the top floor of a building— freefall—hit the ground. *Mom!* I wished—hoped, we could run for it, but we weren't going anywhere.

Logos tried to get a handle too. He tried to shake the chains off, pull them apart, but they were thick and heavy and didn't care about us. He tried to catch his breath, with his back against the wall, knees bent, hands on top, to think. He did it often, and it came off like he didn't give a crap to those who didn't know him. It didn't matter, I knew him. It's how he solved problems, by running all the possibilities through his head. Don't get me wrong, he was scared all to hell, too.

There was no one around to help us. No family, or friends, or police were coming. We were in the air, in a cargo plane which made a prison, and still, I shook. If one thing was sure, there was no turning back now. Maybe it was the right plane, or we were the right men on the wrong plane, but man, we were on it either way.

We tried to pull the chains, tried to talk, tried to imagine who would do this to two young blokes. Why? What in the hell did we do to anyone, really? We had always minded our own business, and went on this job contract overseas, where we could put bankruptcy and tough times behind us to make bank. We were supposed to be at a mine in Peru for the next six months as the head of maintenance.

Neither one of us was important, nor rich, as far as I knew. Some did blab Logos had the mind of Tesla but for mechanics, fixing anything with an engine and all. Yeah, they were right about it, as I saw firsthand what he could do. He might make up to three million per year in a profit-sharing agreement. His signing bonus relieved his financial pain, and the assistant got ten thousand per month—not bad.

We sat in the dark hum waiting for the answers Logos said would come. We couldn't stand, the chains had chains, and held us down. There, in the moment, we almost died.

But we didn't die, and I kept on thinking about what my dad liked to say, "Believe what you see, not see what you believe." It's what I called kitchen apron philosophy; the kind of thing which would be embroidered on a mother's kitchen apron in cursive while she ran around baking or scrambling up some eggs. It made no sense to think about it in our predicament, but his words helped me get through it. Those things always killed me, man, because they worked all the time. No matter the hell, I kept seeing the cursive on the apron.

§

I tried to get all the clues from the space I could, but the dim, and my pounding heart, didn't help. The fear blinded me. What is it they always say? Each person must conquer a fear for them to grow up. What if the fear itself is what needed conquering? I thought about it my whole life. "The mind, fear is in the mind," I could hear Father Manso saying in class. I never understood it. I'd have to conquer it, now, or it would eat me alive in this place, or wherever we'd end up.

The three large crates sat in a row in front of us. I extended my legs through one of the gaps separating them. Strips of black non-slip tape covered the floor all down the passageway like lane dividers on a highway. I tried to get up again and got pulled right back down. Oh crap, I bit my nails to the skin.

The plane leveled out. A young man with a rifle, in full brown camos, came over and pulled out the gags from our mouths. We yelled at him, but he walked away toward the cockpit.

I looked at Logos. "W...what in the hell's going on?" Man, my heart was pounding like crazy.

Logos's eyes ran around the space. "Snatch job."

"*Why?*"

He shook his head. "I'm working on it."

"What's going to happen? Where are we going?"

He didn't know, yet.

The future had become the present—the slow second-by-second present. I couldn't see beyond it, and everything I ever dreamed of becoming was gone.

Logos tried to get a handle of the situation, too. "Let me do the talking."

We couldn't see a goddamn thing in the dim. Somewhere within the cabin, a whistle grew hypnotic and into heavy breathing, and phlegm clearing a nasal passage, phlegm and breathing, in and out, in and—

"Who's there?" Logos said.

"The guide." The sick phlegm became a voice. "We have you." A dark face cut out of the air between the crates.

"Who are you? Get these things off us, *now*!"

He made us wait. "I am *Mr.* K. K." He spoke with a French accent. "We have you."

"For what?"

"You fix the temple."

Logos and I stared at each other.

"What?" Logos said.

Brilliant teeth seeped from across the dim. The man wore a chain of enormous crocodile teeth around his neck—and it wasn't attached to him—no, he was attached to *it*. The contour of his body wrapped around the chain like a dark sleeping bag. He sat, legs bent, one over the other, one hand over each knee; an idol, trinket, or Black Buddha flying coach.

"Where're we going? Tell me!" Logos demanded.

"To the mine. Central Africa."

What's, where's, and how's pressed their way from our lips.

"Fuck no!" I said. I tried to stand and crashed back down. "It's Peru. You can't do this."

"Do not fight. Do not think," Mr. K. K. said. "We will do this for you, now."

"Let us go," Logos shouted. "*Now*."

The idol shook his head. "We go to DRC, Democratic Republic of the Congo. Far, far away." It lay in the middle of everything, close to nothing. It was his home—our new home, he said, where we would help them re-build a fallen temple to money—the mine.

We demanded to see the pilot.

Mr. K. K.'s attention drifted. "I remember it—Belgian Congo. Later, Mobuto rename—Zaire. Now, the DRC." He recited it slow and deliberate, like a doctor telling a patient how long they have to live. "No go to Peru. We go mine in Kivu territory. There you will work. Both of you." He glanced at me. "Hard work for white men."

In my freshman year at Villiers Military Academy, a senior prick came up from behind me in the hall one day and sucker punched me right in the gut. I couldn't breathe. I folded over and thought I was about to die. Every word coming from Mr. K. K.'s lips felt like that day.

"It's kidnapping," Logos said. He tried to think. "To do what there, exactly?"

"They never tell me." He cleared the phlegm from his throat. "Perhaps to see if you are the great man they say."

Logos pulled at the chains. "Take these off."

"But I never met a great man in my life."

Logos didn't flinch. "Until today."

Mr. K. K. waved him away, pressed a switch, and a maintenance bulb lit his jaw white-hot. His face twisted up like a wet towel. Pock marks plotted a line from his temple down to his mandible, and a dent in one jowl plunged deep enough to nearly touch the other.

"We will see. I am driver, I know nothing."

"You said *guide*," Logos said.

"I am everything to you." His gaze froze on us. We became his objects, part of the inventory the loadmaster needed to track.

The other guard came back. He was a boy, really, a young snotter given a rifle as a toy, adult camos, and too many pats on the back. He stood over us with the key, patted his rifle for us to see, and unlocked the chain to the wall and manacles from our hands for us to use the can. The chains on our feet remained.

Logos jumped up and knocked on the cockpit door for a solid minute with no answer. I came over, kicked the door hard, and knocked until my hand went numb. I looked out the window seeing only clouds below, so flat, I could walk on them back to New York. We could all walk back.

It raged inside me. The old wrath, like a Mr. Hyde couldn't be held back. "This is illegal!" I turned around. "You can't do this." My insides teared. "*Goddamn bastard.*" I clenched my fist and rushed the old man.

I didn't care about the young guard, or the old man and his life, or my family, or friends. A waterfall rushed in a chasm in me, demanding to be filled. Nothing could fill it. Nothing could stop it. Nothing seemed good enough, or right enough, or strong enough to stop me. I became an army, a colossus, and everything ahead of me would be annihilated. I sensed my anger as the rushing fluid, and fear, its current. It blinded me. I experienced the same damn thing at Logos's repair shop a while back.

Logos recognized it again and stepped in front of me. "Robert, stop."

Mr. K. K. came toward me. His eyes narrowed. He told the young guard to watch.

I unleashed the heavy bomb-hands. They always expect the right hook, so come with the left jab. My left arm came forward, and my fist cracked his nose. I heard it snap. The chains dragged over his head. Blood did the old drip-drip from his nostril, but it didn't stop this prick. He closed his hand around my mouth, clamping my cheeks together. It pushed my nose to one side and my gums bled. I bombed him again, and the waterfall rushed in a flood inside me, filling me with life.

2

Logos jumped in between us. He kept on saying it was too late. We were in the air—we're in it. We couldn't go back. This was the reality of now and all. I still fought to get at the old prick, but Logos wrangled me with his one arm. I couldn't move. His arms were as thick as legs from the years of mechanical work.

The guard watched and laughed, and Mr. K. K. laughed too, dabbing his nostril with a napkin.

I wouldn't accept any of it. "I'll tear that mother—"

"No, you won't," Logos said. His lips bent into a hard line. He scanned the tracks of scars over Mr. K. K.'s body and knew the map. He pulled me back. "He's seen more wars than your little prick."

He told me to breathe, to think, to see the plane, the old man, the situation—there wasn't anything else. It was too late. I did what he said, I came back to myself, to this reality.

I guess it's why they had sent me off to the most revered lump of bricks in Montreal, Villiers Military Academy, the VMA. It's where they taught us boys how to control the old wrath, and in the meanwhile, be molded into young men. When Dad sent me, it didn't go over well. It was the first time I was away from home, but like everything, with enough time, we learn to adjust. I dealt with it, so I had to deal with this now. A year ago, my parents had to do the old bankruptcy dance with the attorneys, and it turned to shit, too. I'll get to it all later. For now, Logos reminded me of Dad, acted like him, but knew more. He always knew more than anyone. I didn't understand it.

§

"Calm, my friends," Mr. K. K. said, charm offensive in play. "We let you walk because you cannot run. So, calm, for now."

We understood, loud and clear. We couldn't get to the cockpit, we couldn't turn around, we couldn't parachute off, we couldn't fight the little shit camo who had a rifle, and what looked like a Kalashnikov. We had to accept it for now, and we did, slowly.

The old man tilted his head back to dab his nose. He looked over at me, wooden smile, dead eyes seeing a forgotten chore. The eyes scolded, embraced, and everything fell inside of them. They could change with no rhyme or reason.

"You look so *se-ri-ous*," Mr. K. K. said. He broke out in laughter. "Soon, I show you my country."

Logos leaned close to me. "Don't do it again. No help coming, got it? Keep your, *I want to live my dreams* crap for your father or girlfriend."

A rush of shame came over me. Everything blurred, not where it should be. Everything I learned from him seemed wasted. He taught me the important stuff, to think for myself, everything I'd need when we got to this new place to succeed. We were supposed to be repairing excavators and such at a gold mine in Peru. For the first time in my life I would be making my own money, and man, how I needed it to save my family.

Mr. K. K. kept an eye on me. He shifted his gaze to the cargo, to Logos. "You are mechanic?"

"Field technician," Logos said.

"Yes, the *mechanic*." He laughed again, and his one cheek almost collapsed into the other. "They wait for you there."

Villagers, workers, politicians, military, even the guys scrubbing the grimy dishes clean, stood idle waiting for a man to arrive. He said this man knew how to fix everything, fix equipment the size of dinosaurs. He needed to repair their *temple*, some ineffable structure in the middle of a field which produced diamonds. Like the bread and wine of communion, oh, how they needed some for the sacrament. He put it this way: fix the temple, feed his village, fill the coffers, and perhaps, glut a nation. Only one man could do it and I was with him.

"I want to speak to David from the Consortium," Logos demanded.

"Who?"

As for our employer, we never got anything more than the name on the brass doorplate: Consortium Partners II, Ltd, as the payor on the checks. A little jockey of a man, named David, whom we met only a week ago, signed them. Logos accepted three hundred thousand as a signing bonus—verification enough, and I came along as his assistant. Good pay, see the world, have an adventure, they said.

Mr. K. K. swung his chin my way. "You? His bodyguard?" A speck of blood still shined below his nostril.

I shook my head. I wanted to say something to him—anything—a jab to ruffle him further, but my head still spun. Logos could tell. He squinted at me to shut-up until I blinked consent.

Not even six months ago, I donned a robe, threw up a cap; first NYU class of '94. After the bankruptcy, and no job prospects, this whole thing came about. What a turn.

"What needs fixing?" Logos asked. "Mining equipment?"

"Rest now, my friend."

"No *friends*, only clients."

"Maybe it's why you in this plane, alone, thinking you go to Peru." He gave the old wooden smile, again.

No one said anything for a long time. My old life was over, man, really over.

§

Our eyes adjusted to the dim. It clarified the other cargo contents: two dozen steel poles, smelling of new grease and oil, stretched the length of the fuselage. Mr. K. K. used them as a bench. A laminated spec sheet, tagged to the poles, danced back and forth with the movements of the plane. Several long black duffel bags lay next to them, locked from the zipper to a loop on one end. Nothing appeared marked for contents, but everything lay sealed shut by red security tape, including the three crates.

The twisted napkin hung in Mr. K. K.'s his nose like a bloodied stalagmite.

"Much work to do." His voice ran monotone. "Things bad." He didn't care how the message came out. "You will see." He was a man void of those things we thought came stock, like vanity, fantasy, or finesse. "We will see the kind of man you are, my friend."

"It's an abduction," Logos said. "You'll be the first on trial, *my friend*. Now, tell us what in the hell's going on here?"

"Okay, you mad. I see." He cleared his nose. "The people wait for you. We see what you can do when the time comes. Relax, now."

"Who sent you?"

Mr. K. K. rubbernecked to the wall. "Sleep. Twenty hours to DRC."

§

We got up and tried the cockpit door again.

The boy guard watched, knowing it was hopeless. He never slept. Each time his eyelids crept down, he popped a few pills, and became his old vacant self. He chained us back up.

I fell asleep, and I don't know for how long. I went into it deep, and time stretched and coiled. I dreamt about my old room at my parent's house in Montreal. I had this old faux oak bed, where I cut out Wonder Woman Linda Carter from the TV Guide and taped her to the bedpost. Man, I used to stare at her tight superhero outfit all day while I laid down. For some reason, it's what I kept thinking about. I couldn't always control what I thought about and when. I wanted to go back and curl up in my little bed again, forever.

I woke to find Logos asleep, and Mr. K. K. staring cockeyed at him from across the belly of the plane. He kept it up, staring sideways at me too, until he fell asleep, again. I still tasted metallic blood in my mouth.

I dozed off and on for several hours.

§

My stomach sank with the plane's descent. I woke. It was early morning, and everyone else still crashed out. I hadn't slept for more than an hour at a stretch. My body felt beat up like an old gutter pup from the chains, hard floor, and the brawl.

A new world unfolded in the window: an expanse of green-black treetops bulged from the earth and disguised the ground from the poor egrets flying in V-formation. The trees broke up, and silvery water shone through the spaghetti roots as if a saucer turned over, glazing the land.

Logos came to the window, and boots thumped the aluminum behind him. Mr. K. K. stood a few inches from me. His rancid breath hit my neck.

"*Bonjour*, my friends," he said, cheery, all forgotten. He looked over at Logos. "Mechanic, hello."

Something obstructed Mr. K. K.'s breathing, making talking a snore at times. In the morning light, I saw the man in full. A lifetime of harsh repetitive work sculpted cannonball shoulders over two bowed twigs for legs. His face—my god—welted up from a scar which ran from his collar to the cheek. When he breathed, one cheek dented into the other. The rest of him vibrated like a wire. If war marked him, it must've been every war since the Romans.

He looked through the window. "The *Réserve de Chasse de la Léfini*. Big land. We land soon near Kinshasa."

"To deplane?" Logos said, dead tired.

Mr. K. K. said we needed to refuel and later fly to Kisangani. The mine still lay five days drive away.

A river puckered its lips back into the width of the window.

"Congo River," he said. "Brazzaville, Republic of the Congo. Kinshasa, east, in DRC." He moved away. "I sit. We land."

§

We landed on a private strip, like the one we took off from in Pennsylvania. I figured these pricks must've set-up an international network of these to get their people around.

The boy guard still stood by the cockpit door and melted from sweat. He motioned for us to move back.

Mr. K. K. shook his head, and the ivories around his neck twisted. "No one in there," he said, motioning to the door.

"Who flew the plane?" Logos asked.

"The spirits." He laughed.

We told him we want out, now.

He raised his palm. "Quiet, I come back." He dropped from the hatch door and closed it. The guard stayed behind.

We tried the hatch but it remained locked. We waited for a good hour.

§

Logos always wore a black mechanic's jumpsuit, and when he slung his black rucksack over his shoulder, they became one. The pack lay on the ground, and he threw me an uneasy glance when he found his cell phone missing from it. Our passports were gone, too.

It's when the old pumper in my chest ticked. "What's the plan?"

"Not sure but don't lose your cool."

He said he was scared too, but we needed to use this: he tapped his temple, making his shoulder muscles pulse from beneath the jumpsuit. We needed to think, *first*.

Mr. K. K. opened the hatch door and handed us two plates of food. Three bumps lay on each plate: pasty cassava, similar to potatoes, plantains, and a meat carcass. The braised meat looked like a black river stone and wreaked of wild game.

Logos pointed at it. "What kind of meat is this?"

Mr. K. K. shrugged. "Meat."

"No kidding," I said. "What kind?"

"*Meat*."

Logos cast his "meat" aside and I did too. The cassava and plantains filled us up with carbs and our energy returned.

Logos asked the old man about the cell phone and he shrugged back.

Three metal taps clanked against the fuselage. Mr. K. K. jumped up and knocked on the cockpit door three times, paused, twice, and the plane lifted off.

§

The treetops below grew even larger than before, as if growing on another planet. As the hours passed, they thickened and multiplied into a single breathing organism, hiding the surface, and reclaiming their ownership of the fauna. The trees were the land, and the land was the trees, and where did the land begin, and the green, end?

We put down on a remote strip outside the city. Kisangani was the capital of the *Tshopo* province and located up north. Logos said, in the old-timey days, when British expeditions still keeled over from malaria, they used to call the city Stanleyville, after the great explorer Henry Morton Stanley. Logos had travelled all over the world, seen it all, and knew everything.

Mr. K. K. paced like an expecting father in a waiting room. When the cargo door opened, he wanted to be damn sure he was ready to take on his duties. He told us not to run, as there was nowhere to go. If the plane was a prison, the open land outside made its yard. We'd be driving across it, to the southern Kivu province, where the mine, the workers, and "many important people" waited for the cargo, and the main man to arrive.

Logos could see I was shivering like a rabbit. Wherever we ended up, and whatever they wanted Logos to do, we might end up as dead men. We had to think about a way out.

"When the door drops," he said, "be ready for hell." His eyes ran over the fuselage, the old man, the crates, me, and the door. "We're going through the Fourth World, deep into the shit."

I realized our lives were in Logos's hands. I had to ask: "Are we going to be okay?"

He didn't answer.

"Think you can fix it all when we get there?"

He held out his hand. "It's on me."

There was no turning back. I shook it with everything inside me.

The props tapered off. A whiny motor came on. The old pumper in my chest raced when the cargo door opened.

3

Congolese men rushed in, unlatched the crates, checked documents, and removed everything. Each man wore a T-shirt, with camouflage pants over heavy black boots. Fourteen of them, counting the forklift driver, moved about, some lifting the crates out. Their skins shined, tightened over their sharp bones. Each man knew exactly what to do.

Mr. K. K. reminded us about not running and repeated the miserable rap about the giant prison yard waiting outside, where we couldn't run, even if we wanted to. He told the young snotter guard to unlock all the chains. The old man checked on us every few minutes, shifting his head our way at regular intervals.

"We go," Mr. K. K. said.

A rush of wet sunlight baked the cabin and we sweat. We thought about making a wild dash, but with all the camo men around, the young prick holding his Kalashnikov, and the old prick watching us bake, yeah, this was as good as any prison yard.

"Drink." The old man handed us bottles of water. He picked up his bags. "Go to truck." His palm cut a "C" out of the air for us to move. "Go!"

The trucks waited for us. Five three-axle heavy-duty haulers parked in a convoy, engines idling. They were all painted dark green like the treetops seen from the air. We had to move.

I took a deep breath. I stepped on another continent for the first time. I never saw the sky so blue, the trees so thick and green, and black with cover. Sawgrass waved in the breeze, feathering the mountain ridge. It could have been like any other place, except it was a new place, a faraway place, desolate and yet a grasp away.

High-boned Congolese men walked by taking us in, all talking with the same accent as Mr. K. K. When they spoke English, the voices were nasally, wrapped in a French accent. They spat in the dust when they looked at us, and their gazes left me empty inside. I looked at Logos and realized for the first time—*we* were the strangers. They walked on, whispering fragments, slipping on the damp soil. Brown mud as thick as wet concrete started where the asphalt ended, turning their black boots gray.

§

Mr. K. K. watched the men load one 8' x 8' crate into each of the three longer trucks. If anything in their work ran slowly, it was the handling of the crates. There was something precise and surgical about the transfer, as no bumping, or dropping would be tolerated. An efficient human machine clicked on, as the loading of the other equipment followed. All the Congolese men now held rifles.

"What in the hell?" Logos murmured to himself.

I still had trouble breathing.

Mr. K. K. swept a smile over us. He was a new man in the body of an old man now. The idol floated, felt reborn on familiar land. His black irises expanded, as he moved in his element, in the green.

"You, there. Him there," Mr. K. K. said. He motioned for us to get into one of the shorter trucks, the lead truck.

He walked behind us, half shepherd, half guard.

We were traveling—sure, into the depths of gloom—certified. They needed Logos for something, and it gave us enough air to breathe. Yet, his voice strained at times. He couldn't hide it.

I asked him if we got conscripted.

"No," he said. "We're slaves."

"W...what?"

Someone ripped the earth from beneath my feet, and I went down, falling down I went, but I never hit bottom, only my stomach hit bottom, and my heart, and everything I once dreamed and planned and hoped for crashed down.

Logos looked over my shoulder. "We'll be made to work like slaves." He bit his lip. "There's a war, too," he said. "We're headed close to Rwanda, where it's at. It's all I know." He took a nervous breath.

We kept walking—marching, really, without realizing it. Looking at the convoy, it reflected the sort of trek he described: days long and into the shit.

A feeling of dread came over me, even worse than the plane ride. On the plane, I couldn't see the future, as the present, and our lives, inched along the narrow moment. Now, we could see things coming: the men, the bush, the work, but dread always feels the same, because the time to improvise and get the hell out of it, has already past. Something was coming. It couldn't be stopped.

Mr. K. K. came up from behind. "Move."

We asked where the mine was, and to our surprise, he gave a few crumbs.

The Kivu Equatorial Mine, KEM, near Kindu, in the southeast, waited for us. It waited with open arms like some newbie mom adopting an orphan. There we would work, eat, sleep, and listen to them.

We demanded to speak to David from the Consortium, first, and got back a look of aliens landing on his planet, and to shut the hell up.

"Man, maybe my English no good?" he said.

"It sucks," Logos said, testing him.

Mr. K. K. raised his bony finger to Logos's face. He pointed to the truck.

Nothing else happened, and it told us something: they needed us—Logos, more than Mr. K. K. was willing to say. When they need you, man, you really got something there. They can't waste you for nothing because they can't get from you what they need. We needed to remember it.

Logos understood it better than I did. Although he folded into himself at times, he guided us the best he could. I was damn glad he was there.

§

Whew! Whew! Whistling came from behind us. A tall Congolese man clicked his chin hello to Mr. K. K. "Boss, all ready to go." A long thin neck gave the impression of his head and neck being one.

"This Izbart," Mr. K. K. said. "My number one." Mr. K. K. threw his chin at Logos. "This the man."

"Yes?" Izbart shifted his attention between them like watching a tennis match. "I have great honor to meet you, sir." He straightened his back, extended his hand to shake. Sweat covered it, but Logos shook it and didn't care. Izbart nudged Mr. K. K. to notice. "Many wait for the great man to come. Thousands."

"Great men do not exist." Mr. K. K. said, "only hardworking men, who make other men rich. We need to go."

"Please, try the best," Izbart said. He tried to read Logos.

"I don't know anything about this," Logos said "I'm only a man, like you."

Izbart nodded.

Engines revved, and wheels slipped in the silt. Some of the men talked and smoked.

Mr. K. K. withdrew a museum-piece Kalashnikov from his bag. He stood it upright, pointing and moving it as an extension of his arm. He snapped in a magazine with a baby-bottom pat. When the magazine clicked into place, the men went back to work.

All the men carried such rifles, frayed muzzle to butt. I wondered could they even fire.

Mr. K. K. took the wheel of the lead truck. He pointed for us to sit directly behind him in the cabin. Izbart climbed into the passenger seat. The other drivers shook their hands in a frenetic symphony, and moved from the air, to drumming the roof tops, to roll out.

Mr. K. K. plunked down the clutch—bang. It felt good to move on the ground after being in the air for so long. We moved, and saw things, and stayed alive. It wasn't much but better than death. I remembered the prick driver, and the airstrip, and signing our Death Benefits Form in the back of the car. *Son of a bitch.*

§

Driving through Kisangani, smiling billboards for Air Afrique and Coca-Cola lined up one after the other, red hues bleached pink, the blacks gray. Whitewashed brick buildings buckled and leaned and could be sucked back into the bowels of the world at any time. Farther out, the pavement turned to dust.

Mr. K. K. read over his map, smoked, and drove all at the same time. When he put the map down on the center console, it sat folded. I studied it as much as I could.

A tiny manufacturer's badge on the glove compartment faced

Izbart: *VLRB, Véhicule de Liaison et de Reconnaissance Blindé*. All the trucks were armored, or at least ours. I nudged Logos to see it.

We drove on, seeing the greener countryside, less of the tattered buildings.

§

On the outskirts, the junkyards popped up; shantytowns of corrugated metal cut out from the hillside, making a suburbia. One metal cubicle hung over the other, leaned over the other, the rust running like tears. Laundry hung and bowed on the lines, and gaunt women pulled the hardened cloth into baskets, and the baskets became heavy, pulling down the women, and bowing their spines into question marks.

Things smoothed and calmed on the N3 National Highway. It appeared like any rural asphalt road in Canada or America with mountains to look at. Trees clustered around high open areas on the sides of the road, and the mountains and trees went on forever, and the sun hung over, bright and hard and always there, boiling the horizon. The road ran on, and the quiet followed, leaving the still and old behind us in the rearview mirror. It was unforgettable, and we felt it, but we wanted to forget it. We pushed on.

The old man only knew two ways to drive: too fast or too hard on the stoppers. When we were forced to slow down, he would pound the wheel. When the road cleared, and his foot found clearance on the gas pedal, he sang.

Oh, bé-bé-bébé.
Oh, wh-wh...why
you so-so-young?

He surprised me he could put all his congestion aside to belt out a tune—any tune. My jab may've even improved his resonance.

"You look my map," he said to me. He pointed outside to the horizon. "Mine is far from every direction."

I couldn't actually see the map's legend or judge distance of any kind. Eyeballing it, the KEM sat fifty, even a hundred miles east of Kindu, in an undeveloped green patch.

"Only two ways in," Mr. K. K. said, laughing. "Every time you start in one direction, you wish you would have gone in the other." He giggled like an old kid who'd found a skin mag on the playground.

§

More driving, and no one wanted to move, much less speak.

I thought about my family. I was sorry for making their lives hell. I was an unruly soul at times, and it got me sent to the military academy for it. Now, the one thing I feared more than being kidnapped, was never seeing them again. *Mom, Dad, I'm sorry I got myself into this. I'm sorry for everything I put you through, and the time when the police came that afternoon. I did stupid things when I should've done smart things and should've listened, but I talked, instead. Maybe I deserved it. This time, I got what I feared. I'm sorry.* I was a twenty-one-year old kid, and what was the purpose of everything I'd ever done?

§

Logos didn't brood as much. He kept on thinking. He saw an opportunity and inched forward. "Hey, what's in the crates?"

I'm glad he asked. Something told me our future—or lack of it—shifted inside them.

"For the mine," Mr. K. K. said into his rearview mirror. He had made us a magnanimous gift, and we should shut up now. He made some all-knowing nod. "Our business."

Izbart half-turned to us, "We carry equipment over ten million dollars US in those—"

Mr. K. K. snapped his fingers at Izbart. "Quiet you. No more." He looked at both of us. "No more."

We asked about the road trip instead.

Izbart craned his neck to us. It moved as if on a swivel. We should make Kindu in three days but to resupply only, he said. It would take two more days to the KEM, as the roads became dust, and the convoy would need to move even slower to keep the cargo safe. They would keep to the schedule barring any pirates or hijackers.

I exchanged glances with Logos.

"Ten million dollars' worth of what?" Logos said.

Mr. K. K. split a grin. "Wouldn't you like to know."

4

On the outskirts of nowhere, a hermaphroditic figure waved to us. We slowed to see a table spread before him, a barrel barbeque to his side. It was bushmeat drive-thru: monkey, snake, boars, and feral cats hung on a clothesline, or crackled on the grill. It sold everywhere. Street hawkers tried to move it smoked, grilled, boiled, barbequed, even breathing. It made me sick.

Mr. K. K. reveled in our disgust.

We rolled out.

Logos slipped his hand into his rucksack by his leg and withdrew a detailed sketch of what looked like an old-fashioned oil well derrick. He held it down, careful not to draw any attention. I recognized it as a rendering from a diagram in the book *Core Drilling* I brought along from the library, to jumpstart my career in mining maintenance. They called it the "A-frame" or "headframe" structure. He took a pen out and continued to sketch, drawing a circle around the drill rod, and starring it. He studied the section for hours. Considering a human hand did it, the steadiness of the lines blew me away.

Something felt odd. We were off the goddamn plane, unshackled, and out here in the big "prison yard," but a sense of shame had seeped in. We felt less than before, less than men. We couldn't think as before, to run, to feel, to plan, and dream. Others did it for us now, as Mr. K. K. predicted. We weren't whole, and each man tried to hide it.

§

The road bent like a plumber's fitting; right, and left, finally heading southwest. The truck's bulky treads hummed over the roadway. At first, they went *ump-thump, ump-thump, ump-thump,* until the senses adjusted to the noise, and the noise became a continuous hum.

A line of people, holding sheet sacks over their shoulders, hugged the road. Everyone in the trucks looked at them.

"Hutu refugees from Rwanda," Izbart said. He shook his head. "More every day."

Some of the people were missing hands, or feet, or limbs. Women pulled along children by a tether on their waistband, and the children pulled along goats, and all plotted along in no particular hurry. We sped up, and the line of humans kept on growing.

"There are NGOs which help," Izbart said. "The government try their best, too."

Mr. K. K. scoffed, and his bad breath filled the cabin. "Why you talk to them?" he said to Izbart.

Izbart shrugged.

Mr. K. K raised his forefinger. "I tell you about the government. I know them. I show you." Something boiled inside of him. "You see?" He pulled his collar down. "Look."

A gray worm-like scar winded its way down from his face to the middle of his chest; the scar I'd seen on the plane. It welted up high, like a mountain range growing out of a man.

"They got him," Izbart said.

"*Quiet,* I speak. Force Publique almost kill me when I was a boy. They *almost* kill me, but no, they no kill—K.K. no easy kill. They say I steal the cigarettes. They have no proof. They point to me to stop. They say, 'Give back or you will hurt.' I make the decision which change my life. I say, 'I *choose* to hurt.' They slice me with *la bayonet,* here." He pushed down on the welt. "From this time, I live in the streets, in the bush, wherever. I know them. Where they go. Where they no go. Where we go—nothing go there."

§

We kept on, and the motors kept on, and the tires rolled on, and the road, too. Nothing would stop us. The strip of asphalt went on, always there for us, always offering more of itself for those with the will to take it. After a while, the asphalt and the convoy seemed to collapse into a single point in the windshield, and we became the road, and the road became us.

Logos slept and kept his hand over his rucksack. Mr. K. K. would look at him too often and for too long in the mirror. Izbart looked at him as well. I wondered what they were thinking about.

I kept reading *Core Drilling,* I learned about stitch, deep, and large diameter hole drilling, and tectonic plates, rock-types and reservoirs, and stresses, and horizontal wells, directional wells, and more stresses and hostile places, where not every drill-man came back at all. Oh, I forgot to mention, of the types of rocks mentioned in the book, they complained about the igneous rock, most; rock once molten, which cooled like granite. The hardest to crack, they said, and called it the "bitch rock."

Did we think of attacking Mr. K. K. or Izbart as we drove, and crashing the truck, and trying to get away? Hell yes. But we would be mangled like old gutter pups under the tires, and over the asphalt, and be caught. They also had guns and we didn't. It was dumb, man, dumb, dumb, dumb, but we thought about it.

§

The sun beat down on us when we pulled into Kindu. It looked like the outskirts of an Old West set, but Izbart informed me we sat in downtown central. Patches of grass made sidewalks which weren't there, and a gust of wind lifted the dust out and away. Something beckoned the passerby to its trails and crumbling wood buildings, and to a single dirt path which dragged the shacks like a rug being pulled from under. Nothing appeared to have ever changed in this place. It was timeless like virtue, vice, or fear.

Our convoy parked across from a large crowd gathered at the market. People fell in and withdrew from the mass, expanding and collapsing the center like a lung. We found the busiest place in Eastern Africa, it seemed.

5
THE NEW OLD WEST

People sat under the general store's portico and sold pots and pans, tarps, and used clothing, all dimmed by the shadow. The burned carcass of a car lay turned over near the store.

Everyone got out, and the camos dissolved into the crowd. The gun boys remained, watching over the cargo, over us.

"Remember," Mr. K. K. said. "We let you walk because you cannot run."

I wanted to sprint for it. To hell with it all, I'd risk it now. But a brown camo guard shadowed us the whole way. He was a kid too, probably no more than eighteen, and eager to show the other boys what his rifle could do. He stayed a few yards behind us at all times, and we made sure not to walk too fast.

I turned around and perused the things for sale outside: a cracked lantern without a wick or burner, cracked jerrycans, gauze, a yellowed prosthetic foot. (Caucasian for some reason.)

Near the convoy, nuns in brown monastic habits, boarded a school bus. The bus's engine went *click click click!*

Logos stood by watching.

A blond woman, with fair skin and open blue eyes, came over from the white vans parked next to the school bus. She waved to the bus driver and stepped up inside. An older man followed her. He wasn't old, but older than Logos, who was thirty-five. The older guy and woman wore matching T-shirts, printed with a powder blue cross on the breast. It was a uniform, really; *Médecins Assistance International (MAI)* printed on the backside.

I called for Logos, but his gaze froze on the fair lady before him.

He stepped up on the front bumper, opened the hood, and got the engine started.

The blond woman came out holding a closed umbrella. "We're appreciative," she said. An English accent lengthened each syllable. "*All* the ladies are appreciative." She motioned to the school bus, where the nuns filled the windows.

She was natural, without make-up, or sharp features, or pomp. Her face calmed everything in its orbit.

Logos cleaned his hands, fidgeted, breathed too hard for too long. It was funny to see him this way.

Our immediate reaction was to spill our guts to the first person and get help but we didn't. The guard stood behind us the entire time. With all the new people around, it felt strange for him to be there, and for old Uncle Kalashnikov to be watching over his shoulder. And there was the shame to deal with, too. It weighed, and I knew Logos felt it.

"A fellow traveler helping out," Logos said.

"Well, we work here, Sebastian and I, and the ladies." She looked over at the old guy.

"Sebastian Ramirez," he said, with a Spanish accent.

His face was smooth and round, but crow's feet made their mark. Salt and pepper hair fell into his eyes, which he pushed away. He was the *lead* doctor at MAI, and the way she talked about him, it sounded like a prestigious gig. We shook all around.

She looked at our parked convoy. "Government contractor, of sorts?"

The thought of telling someone else what happened, or passing a note, left the fear of innocent people being hurt. Instead of lying, Logos asked about MAI.

Ramirez stepped closer to her, as if she may run away.

"We're chartered to assist refugees in a conflict," he said. "But everyone is helped." He looked at her. "We should get going." He moved toward the vans.

"Doctor, dear, I'll be along." She smiled, and her clear blue eyes pinched at the corners like a Persian cat.

He gave us a full visual pat-down and moved on.

In the bus windows, the nuns hung their arms out making soap bubbles with empty magnifying glasses. Bubbles filled the air, taken away in the breeze.

"Your chaperone?" Logos said, motioning to Ramirez. "Helping out, I understand. A leash, no."

"A fine line does exist. Doesn't it?" she said, raising an eyebrow.

"For the person on the leash it does." He seemed like his old self; the one who fixed my car in his darkened shop in Astoria months ago. Depending on his mood, he could be fun.

"Lord. How true," she said, with a playful pout. "It's sad. I wonder what side I've fallen on?" She put her forefinger to her chin. "Let me see..."

"If you have to ask...it's too—"

"Late. Brilliant!"

We shared a good laugh. We'd tensed up over the trip, never seeing it come. The days since Astoria, NYU, and even VMA, felt like a lifetime ago for me. I'll get to VMA, and the old *attitude adjustment* job they did on me. For now, the present felt new, looked new, and we became new versions of our half-selves in it. It felt good to enjoy something—anything, and we could laugh in this space suspending whatever future we knew was coming.

She glanced at the armed camo and asked if there was anything she could do.

Logos said no. He smiled when Congolese children from the market played tag around them.

She made a long *hmm.* "Well, best of luck, I think." Her palm made an airy wave to the parked vans and the two drifted there. "Must get going."

He asked to see her again, and it took her a second to understand why. "Hmm? Oh, Red Cross building if you can get away."

"Right." He nodded and realized something, too. "*If* I can get away."

She sat in the van. "Cheerio. I'm Eden, like the gar—"

"Garden."

She shook her head, creasing the corners of her eyes. Ramirez whispered something to Eden. The vans pulled away, followed by the school bus.

As he walked in front of me, I realized I didn't know diddly-squat about him besides his age. In the beginning, he fixed my car, and I helped him investigate a business issue and contract, which got us both shanghaied here. In turn, he offered to bring me along on so I could make some bank. It dawned on me, this guy always kept quiet, especially about anything personal. I realized it was a skill of his. I'd flip it on him. Thou who dig for treasure, shall find.

6

The convoy had parked next to a shuttered bazaar straight out of Lawrence of Arabia. There were Arabic arches and pinched crests and old paint, which peeled off and parachuted like cottony dandelions over the dark huddled forms which slept beneath its arcade.

I leaned on the wall thinking about my ex-girlfriend, Lauren, my parents, and wondered if I'd ever see them again. I can get as sentimental as a girl sometimes, and I hid my tears.

Things had changed for the shanghaied, though. The future was the present, getting through each moment, and staying alive. All those dreams of mine to be an entrepreneur, help out my family, buy a cool pad, and maybe start my own family one day, had been wiped out. I thought about making a mad dash into the bush, again, until the idea evaporated along with the rest, as the brown camo stood by. *God damn it.*

I walked over to Logos. "These people who sent us here, you ever met them before?"

"No." He kept on walking.

"How did they find you?"

He stopped. "Some guys came by the shop one day and told me about it."

Something always told me this guy was in the intelligence business in the past, as some secret agent, or something seen only in a movie. I needed to know, and I came prepared this time. "You never talk about the past. You deflect people from ever getting to know you. Why?"

"Things in the past are past. Dwelling on it's a lie, an unreality."

"W—what?"

"By thinking of the past, you deny reality. You're lying to yourself. It's simple."

I breathed. My dad had always said, each man has taken a different road than you. Be thoughtful, and never assume to know a person without knowing their story, first. To know them, watch them, listen. I decided to listen.

"Honesty is the refusal to fake reality," he said.

When someone lied, they pulled in those around them to perpetuate the lie—to make their unreality true, like I was trying to do to him now.

"Got it, I think." I wasn't completely sure, but the guards distracted me. They gathered by the trucks and stared. Sometimes they laughed at us. "What in the hell are we going to do now?"

"I'm working on it."

I kept thinking, run for it—go, run into the bush, risk a shot by Uncle Kalashnikov into my back, where I would fall face first into the red soil, gasp my last breath, and eventually die all alone like an old gutter pup in the weeds. I loved my parents and wanted to see them again. I hoped we'd find a way out.

§

Our escort motioned for us to come back.

I asked Logos why he was always trying to teach me something.

He told me one of the saddest things I ever heard. He never had a friend. Can you believe it? A person had gone through their whole life and never had a friend.

"It's not too late," I said. "You have a friend."

He looked at me. "Who?"

"Me."

He wanted to run away but he couldn't. He didn't. He said he found out too late about friends. "Thanks."

It occurred to me, we could have left earlier, made a run for it, and risked the shot to the back but we didn't. We decided to stay. Our inaction ensured an action: to see this thing through to whatever it was. Logos made the decision for us not to run, and I was there with him. I figured he knew something, or saw an angle, and something changed. If so, he would eventually tell me about it.

The sun dropped, leaving an orange shimmer over the dust path for us to see one last time. We took it in. Our convoy roared down the path as one wiping the town from view.

§

We headed northeast on the last leg to who knows what. After dusk, most of us fell asleep.

The truck stopped a few times during the night. Each time I opened my eyes, my hands got lost in the thick of the night. It penetrated everything, made us prisoners again, as it embalmed its captives in a molasses, dark, sour, and quiet.

The next morning, a mountain range came up.

Izbart pointed at it. "We cross the range there."

When we asked what we would be doing at this place we were going, Izbart said there would be hard work, important work, work which would change thousands of lives. It involved mining equipment, which Logos needed to fix. Izbart hoped for a change at the mine. Mr. K. K. told him to shut the hell up, again.

We kept on rolling, kept on chugging, kept on worrying each turn would be our last. When we thought the last turn came, it didn't, and we stayed alive. We were alive because they needed us—or Logos—more alive than dead. It was my own theory and gave me hope.

§

The savannah came up, red oat grass, and thin acacia trees, which tunneled over the road to see the apricot sky through a keyhole. Nothing else moved; nothing else breathed. Only the wind told us the rest of the world still ticked away somewhere.

Whoosh. Over a hill, the truck's hood dove and turned my stomach.

Mr. K. K. came alive. "The mine!"

I saw the outskirts of the KEM for the first time.

6

THE NOTHING

A new asphalt road split the plain like a suture. On the shoulders, slivers of men, with wire frames, waited for a parade. Some looked like they hadn't eaten in months, only bones stacked on other bones. The frames pushed out from the fibers of skin, and veins pushed out from their legs, and bellies bloated from empty guts. Some wore arms slings made of twine. The truly depleted, hid their condition beneath junked flour bags made of gunny sack, draped shoulder to knee. Thousands of men waited, all broken men, all cog and wire machines.

They looked beyond Mr. K. K., beyond Izbart, even ignoring the whole raucous convoy. They stood on their toes to see into the depths of the cabin. Some men even sat on the shoulders of others, chicken-fight style, coming close to our lead truck to peer inside. One underling lost his footing, and sent the top man skidding off our door on Logos's side. They fell backward onto the grass, and everyone along the road laughed. Yes, they risked their lives to see Logos. It was an amazing sight.

Logos noticed they wanted him, but he kept mum, still raveled up within himself.

"Look like you the man today," Mr. K. K. said.

"Why?" Logos said.

Mr. K. K. looked at him in the center rearview mirror. He gave Izbart permission to fill us in without giving too much away.

The mine sat idle. It waited for a man to fix the rot, give it CPR, a blood transfusion, and such. He needed to revive not only the mining equipment, but everything peripheral to the production on the premises. There was only one man to do it—Logos. Like a long awaited train pulling into a station, his reputation preceded arrival and had spread. Before we ever got here, he was known in the industry as a mine turnaround expert. Now he'd be tested to see if myth made man, or man made myth, or man equaled expectation, or something. Izbart made it sound as if Logos could lay his hands on everything, and it'd come to life. It would begin when we talked to Chicotte.

"He supervisor, the boss man," Izbart said.

The crowd grew near the gatehouse, gathering around Logos's side of the cabin.

"Workers," Izbart said. "Live in the village there." He pointed to a low tree line in front of us where smoke corkscrewed out. "They say a great man come to change the way of this mine."

"They no say great," Mr. K. K. said. He was raging. "He no great. I never meet great man in my life—I never will."

"What he, sir?"

Smug lips mugged into the rearview. "He *think* he great."

Logos winked at me.

Izbart looked back at Logos and extended his hand for a shake. Logos gripped it.

Two concrete pillars rose from the land and marked the gate. A nervous hand had scrawled "KEM" on each. A wall, with barbed wire atop, ran as far as the eye could see. Watchtowers stood above everything like lighthouses without a sea.

Congolese guards in blue camos waved us by.

§

The forest had been cut down. The last of the tall trees grew out of murky ponds. Men and women, soaked all the way through, dug into the terrain, which resembled wet rice paddies, reddened from the silt. They panned the flooded soil, and their wet T-shirts clung to them. Out came rocky sands, sifted to filter the heavy particles out. Children worked too, panning next to the adults; feeble colts not more than ten years old. Armed camos stood by, watching the sands swirl in the pans, and for diamonds to stay out of pockets, or orifices, or holes in the ground.

"The crap miners," Mr. K. K. said.

"*Artisan* miners," Izbart said. "From village. Work this way because main equipment not working."

A man with his tiny son slept together in fetal positions on the edge of one of the ponds. It broke your heart, man, it really could.

"Lazy dogs," Mr. K. K. said. He coughed and lit a cigarette.

Izbart said the people of the village tried the best they could under the circumstances. What were those, *exactly*? There were no tools, no machines, no automation to help them. Why did the people look and act this way? Management only provided enough food and water to fight the heat, waters, and those camos hovering over every dulled stone in the pans. It was slow, but some volume came out of the ground.

"Hard work," Logos said.

"Strong backs," Mr. K. K. said.

"They paid well?"

"What the hell you care?" Mr. K. K. turned to us. The eyes looked dead; the spirit behind them died long ago. "They work, eat, work, eat. You see?"

Panning mounds built up and cropped out the thicker forest behind. A man stood on one of them, crisscrossing his arms over his head to Mr. K. K. His bare chest shined as a black mirror in the rays of the sun. Barefoot, in cutoff purple trousers, his long beard and Afro glistened with water.

"K. K.. President of the shit," the man yelled. He looked like the village wise man. "Look! Look—the shit." The man spat in the air at him. "What is this?" He pointed to the ponds, to the men and women and kids panning in the sludge. "Why you allow this, tell me? What will the judge say? *Tell me*."

Mr. K. K. didn't like it, and for some reason, his eyes narrowed on me like on the plane.

I shrugged.

Mr. K. K. pointed his hand at the man like a gun. "Ah. Purple pants, I see you. I will remember you," he said, tapping his temple.

§

We climbed a steep hill. It's when I first saw the steel girding. A high barbed wire fence wrapped the A-frame on a plateau. We faced another gatehouse. The gates opened, and the boom lifted. Ahead, an industrial complex resembling a small-scale oil refinery sat in the middle of nothing.

"This my little town," Mr. K. K. said, pointing to a sign in the median: "*La Petite Ville*, KEM."

The gates slammed shut, jarring us.

Our reason for coming here rose from the flat earth: the shiny steel-girded A-frame loomed over everything like a temple. The black steel housed the drill rod, a long metal shaft which hung from the top of the platform to a few feet over the ground, and ready to pierce the earth. Something told me this tower held our fate.

Beyond the town's plateau hung a veil of mist. It ran as far as I could see into the taller hills, which formed a backrest to the topography. Ponds with worn shrubbery popped up around us, but otherwise we sat on a barren tabletop up to the taller hills. Up there, the hills funneled into a mountaintop so sharp, it scraped the belly of the sky. Dancing around the peak, the mist hung over and hid everything in sight wherever it touched. It came down as a pillar, a monolith, a wall of cold confetti inscrutable to us men on the hard ground. The monolith said nothing, gave nothing. I would call it "the nothing."

The A-frame, or headframe, stood at least fifty feet high. In front of it, an older, shorter, wooden headframe stood in its shadow. Surrounding them, an intricate setup of dirt roads connected enough houses, offices, trailers, and storage sheds for this to be a town. Rusting dump trucks, rock-crushers, tractors with shovels, pick-ups, concrete mixers, jeeps, and giant drill bits, lay strewn. Nothing had been fixed or cleaned for years. Only the new headframe shined.

We stopped in front of a trailer, where the air smelled of fresh paint.

Mr. K. K. pointed at it. "You go now."

We got out. A wet heat ran down my throat along with the paint fumes.

"You go. Chicotte-Bossman, he wait," Mr. K. K. said. "Go."

"Goodbye for now," Izbart said. He became too quiet and blinked warning to us about the trailer.

7
Chicotte

Bells. Church bells rang but not for Mass.
Dozens of gaunt brown camos exited a trailer on cue and marched in a file. They were on a mission, and at this pace, the trucks would be stripped bare in no time. As they marched, their boots scraped off the dry soil cover, which twisted into sheets behind them, up and away. They were the only men around.

"End of the line," Logos said.

We opened the door to the office. Inside, it was a goddamn mess. Behind the thrift store hoard, and foldout desk, and docs stacked on top of chairs, a map showed the perimeter of the property: *4,222 Hectares, KEM*. I figured it for around 10,000 acres and could've been a country within a country. Something rattled and fell.

In the back corner, a large Congolese man leaned on a set of filing cabinets. He could've been an old drill sergeant, or heavyweight wrestler, the way his physique nearly split the seams of his blue camos. This man could inflict tremendous pain if he decided to, but it was lunchtime, his hands were full, and grease slithered down his chops.

"Um, one minute, please," he said, averting his eyes. He was making us wait. He couldn't find a napkin and pulled a document from atop the cabinet instead. He read it, scowled, and wiped his hands with it. "Best napkin I ever read." He went behind the desk. "I am Chicotte. Everyone calls me this." He put out his hand.

Logos stared at it, I shook it, but I didn't want to. We exchanged pleasantries, I think.

Chicotte looked sideways at Logos. "Hold." He brought two chairs wrapped in cellophane from a closet and placed them opposite the desk.

We looked at him to remove the cellophane.

"No knife. Everything new come this month for office. Sit, sit."

We slid off the first time.

Chicotte sat back, smiled, frowned, the whole gambit. "We all here now. Ready for action?" He tapped a framed pic of himself on the desk. In the pic, he wore a military uniform, looked fifty pounds lighter, and thrust his shoulders back. "Me."

"What about Peru?" Logos said, controlling himself. "What in the hell's going on?"

Chicotte raised a finger. "Watch your tongue." He kept up his appraisal. "Things happen in this business. A transfer is normal."

"It's kidnapping. I want to speak to David, or his assistant, Ivan Isavich, now."

He grinned. "Yes, yes. *The Mr. David*. He scary-smart man."

He moved in discrete bits, his final gesture, always amplified and overdone. If he decided to grin, his cheeks leapt too high. If he scowled, they dropped too low. He could dial into some amorphous machine with a menu of emotions on demand.

We told Chicotte we needed a phone, needed to talk to a representative of the Consortium, or a lawyer—any lawyer, or someone from the US Embassy.

He always came back with the boilerplate: "Okay, okay, I tell them after we talk." He curled his bottom lip. "Plenty time for this. Plenty time to call later."

"This is illegal!" I said.

"Quiet, boy." He never even looked my way.

Even if he wanted to call, he couldn't, he said. The telephones didn't work—any of them. The whole mine was shut down. These were difficult times and all, and we needed to move forward. We should understand our employment contract, first. Here it was in his greasy hands, written plain as the day. *Employees may be transferred by employer without prior notice*. Did we see? It was written to cover these mishaps. He shrugged. He told us not to worry, we were still getting paid. When Logos checked his bank account, he would see all the zeros and sleep like a baby cradled in the cash—so don't, don't worry. The telephones? Oh, those would be fixed by Monday, Wednesday at the latest. It was a small detail, he said. He'd seen all this kind of stuff before as the general manager at the KEM, and it always worked out well for everyone, even for the little people like us. How? He was in charge, and the only man qualified to run things—that's how. "The Mr. David," the man himself, had trained him, of course.

We didn't know what the money had to do with it. We were shanghaied, man, and couldn't use it for crap. Things needed clarifying, and I wasn't in the position to be asking.

Logos could see through this crap about a mile away and told him we would confirm all this by Monday. It was Friday again, and five days since we left the US.

§

Well, what to think? We were here, unchained, unharmed, being kept in the dark, being told we were still going to be paid. It meant something, I guess, as we could breathe more. We couldn't run, or hail a cab, or make a call to a loved one to tell them we were fine. What good would money be?

He handed each of us bottles of water. "You make a good drive here?"

"Glorious," Logos said. "I want to do it all over again."

It was bold, and like a good boxer sizing up his opponent in the opening rounds, he landed a blow. Each mocking jab served as a test, probing these pricks to get a sense of the real danger. Every time he did it, I held my breath.

Chicotte wiggled a grin. "We talk, now. Everything is down. Last mechanic, he left. Personal reasons. Not be back."

"How long's it been down?" Logos said, shooting me a glance.

"A few months."

The shut-down looked longer, obvious to any outsider.

"Do not let our dust fool you," he said. "This is major, major mine. *Billions* here." He pressed his index finger against the desk until it bent back. "I say, billions here in La Petite Ville. The diamonds—d'kimberlite pipe from God here."

"What?" Logos asked.

Volcanic activity brought up diamonds in this formation called a kimberlite pipe, he said. He pointed to a piece of paper taped to the map: *Kimberlite Pipe. To be drilled at future Shaft #4*. A cross-section of underground soil layers, shaped like a champagne flute, came out of the center.

He got up. "I show you."

We followed him to a side window, where he showed us the new headframe they built for *Mr*. Logos.

The black steel shimmered in the setting sun. It peered over the old wood headframe, ready to make good on about a billion promises, a billion needs, and dreams. None of those included us, but the fact he called him, "*Mr*. Logos," told me if everything went right, his work might help us buy a one-way ticket out of here.

"They tell me you have the god-hands. Fix equipment for the Shaft #4."

"What equipment?" Logos said.

Chicotte described how the generators and electrical boxes needed fixing, first. The big dinosaur trucks and tractors would come next, followed by the supporting equipment, including the sifters, cars, and carts. The "special installation"—the one they really brought him here for—would come last. He didn't want to talk about it until later. Not to worry, all was taken care of, he said too often. When Shaft #4 broke open this god-pipe, things would change here. The believers would follow the dollars to the temple.

"Inside it have—" Chicotte spread all five fingers. "Five billion dollars inside the stomach."

Logos nodded.

"We build for you." A list of equipment came across the desk. "Hard work for a white man."

I couldn't believe they built the A-frame for him. Neither one of us said a goddamn word. I picked up the list. Dozens of items filled it back and front.

"So it's only me doing the work?" Logos said.

"Some helpers, but you the big ox." He gestured to the desk and chairs. "Let us sit, *fine gentlemens*." He told us we were in the know, part of the "privileged worker-class," compared to the rest of the laborers. Things would still be difficult for us, but some had it worse, and we would see in time. Few men knew what they had there. He knew, David knew, some other people knew, and now we knew. He grew giddy like a child. "We have the god-pipe beneath our feet. Proven." He stomped his boot, and the thin floor wavered on our side.

My heart jumped. "Proven, how?"

Chicotte shifted his eyes to me. "The old hole." He didn't seem too interested in talking to a twenty-one-year-old who hitched a ride with their savior but would oblige and all. "Mine been here long time, but recently we find the proof for the new one." He handed Logos a bound study two inches thick. "We do research, first."

The cover page certified and sealed, "The existence of a rare kimberlitic pipe on the KEM directly accessible from a TBD, Shaft #4." On the last page, stuck another, congruent, with its print obscured. Logos separated the two below the desk line. Chicotte couldn't have known of this second page. Logos read it. He pointed to a single line in the smallest capital letters I've ever seen: IN THE OPINION OF THE GEOLOGICAL SURVEYORS, THIS REPRESENTS A ONCE-IN-A-GENERATION OPPORTUNITY FOR RESOURCE EXPLOITATION.

Logos thought for a moment. "You'll pay me what I ask, when I ask for it."

I almost crapped. What was he doing?

Chicotte waved him off, came around his chair, right up to Logos's face. "Why in the hell I pay you for real?"

"Injure either one of us," Logos said, "and we can't do your work. So, you'll pay me and let us go when I'm done—or nothing gets done." Neither man blinked and time itself stopped.

Chicotte thought about it, pointed at him. "We will see." He pumped his fists. "Ha. I like your style. You are good, good negotiator."

What a relief. He promised Logos they would discuss our exit strategy at a later date. It sounded like crap. He could promise us the world and it didn't matter. We couldn't run.

"A deal," Chicotte said. A paw-like hand stuck out to shake and they did.

Chicotte's eyes shifted between us. When he exhaled, the room filled with an undeniable bouquet of eau de halitosis and liquor. This guy had a few before lunch but couldn't bullshit a bullshitter he was sober. He sweat.

Logos asked Chicotte about the war going on next door. "It's why no one's here?"

Chicotte took his chair again, eased back, slammed his boot on the desk. He could see Logos analyzed where others only listened. He said David was right about him, as he took nothing at face value.

"War is war, the death, the death," Chicotte said. He gave us the skinny: in neighboring Rwanda, the ruling minority Tutsi were under attack by Hutus. The Tutsis went on their own counteroffensive to hold on to their blueblood status. They would sacrifice an entire race to keep it. "Millions die my friend. We...still...here." He paused for effect. "But I do not like the politics. I am only businessman, to give orders."

Logos took a deep breath, too deep for any bull or shit to come out after. "I don't take orders," he said in a calm voice. "I work for myself, only myself."

I glanced over at him to please shut up but he ignored me.

Chicotte nodded to let it go, for now. "You will learn. The men who work for me have learned. I watch everything." His hands cut through the air. "They do everything to make the stone here in La Petite Ville. You can say, I am the mayor."

Logos said he understood. "You have a job to do. So do I. If you let me, I can. But I work for myself, only myself. The satisfaction is mine."

I couldn't see his angle. Maybe he felt it needed to be said, for self-esteem, or self-something. It gave us an inch of freedom, and it's worth more than ten miles chained.

Logos kept jabbing too often, pushing them back too deep. It couldn't last forever. They would come back, and counterpunch, eventually.

Chicotte didn't know what to make of it. A glaze had come over him. He snapped an imaginary stick in two in front of us, as if to say, none of this mattered. Logos could push all he wanted, but they would break us in the end.

At the KEM, there were Masters and Workers. The Masters did their jobs, breaking down men into Workers. The men who became Workers decided when they broke by how much labor they could endure. They decided when to be subjects of the Masters. They did this by handing a Master a broken stick and looking down. Each Master waited for this moment, as there were never enough Workers. When the Workers didn't do as the Masters said, a program ensured obedience. He didn't go into detail about it, but let it hang in the air like some wicked spirit.

Chicotte called obedience "duty," and there was nothing shameful about it; Workers worked, and showed duty; Masters supervised Workers and ensured discipline. It's how things ran when the DRC was the Belgian Congo. It's how it worked today.

Chicotte didn't converse. He recited a shopping list to the help, and we sat and listened.

Thousands of men had come before, with big egos, big muscles, big self-esteems, but none were ever big enough, or strong enough to last. Everyman broke at some point. Some men snapped their sticks in the beginning when they didn't see a way out, and some men put up a fight, because they were used to fighting, and some men saw it was too hard to fight, so they chose the thick yoke around their necks like oxen, to escape the fight. Those who chose to fight—the hard-nosed, hard-headed, too smart, or too dumb for their own damned goods— straightened their backs, looked straight ahead at their captors, and boss- men, and fought not to become Workers, but to remain their own men, never giving up the thing inside of them which made them complete, made them fulfilled men, because they kept their self-esteem protected deep in the pits of their stomachs. Those were the last men to go, he said, but they went too. And all the men fell eventually, and all handed in their sticks to become Workers, even those who fought to work for themselves.

§

Chicotte made a roguish smile which must've charmed the thousands before us who sat across his desk. He told us "fine *gentlemens,*" for now, we could agree to disagree. We needed to move on. He could be charming if he laid off the sauce. It was a dangerous charm because no one knew what aim followed, only him. He could even run for president of the DRC if he used it best.

He stood and steadied himself. "I mean this with all my heart." He placed his palm over his pumper and thought he stood at some imaginary podium looking over his constituents. "We have the best prospects for success of any mining consortium in the world—right here at the KEM." He got choked up and it softened him.

He was sincere, in his own way, and it could make you lay your arms down in war. "We can do the miracle here. The Mr. David says this possible with right person." He placed his hand on Logos's' shoulder and on mine. "I am convinced we have this right person." His hand felt warm, and in the moment, you trusted the warmth even though it was total crap.

Chicotte went to the door. We would begin tomorrow, early, he said.

"Our rooms?" I said. "Need to clean up."

"Oh." He took two steps outside and pointed at the faint white buildings in the dusk. "Go find one." He dialed up a smile. He assured us "five-star arrangements" soon. "Go, *gentlemens*." He looked at Logos. "Big, big surprise party for you tomorrow."

8
Marc

W e stood outside the trailer getting our bearings, as the last daylight
    fell away. The plan: find a spot to crash, stay alive, think of a way
out.

We were unescorted for the first time, and it felt new and exciting.
Did we think about running again, sprinting flat out for an exit? You
better believe it. An armed camo showed up with Uncle Kalashnikov
over his shoulder and squashed those thoughts. He shadowed us
everywhere. Each time we tried to talk to him, he raised the butt of his
rifle. We understood what Mr. K. K. meant when we landed. If the big
land made a prison yard, the KEM plateau made a bigger cell.

The outlines of white trailers shifted between the brush. We went
toward them to find somewhere to crash for the night. A few steps later,
I happened to see a giant hole in the earth.

It sat behind Chicotte's trailer and surrounded us. None of us
stood on a plateau at all. We clung to a manmade precipice on the edge
of the "old hole." It carved out the flat earth and made cliffs. The open
pit diamond mine stretched out to the horizon, and the trailer and Ville
hung on its brim.

A phone rang and we spun around. We headed back toward
Chicotte's trailer. We pulled hard on the door, with no answer. The
brown camo watched us, half-interested.

The hole drew us back. It went on forever, etching its way into the
sky. Pink clouds, sprayed with an orange-tinted collar, hovered over it.
My god—the colors, the colors—I never saw such bright colors before.
I even wondered if the hole made its own weather. Yet, an uneasiness
came from it and stirred up all the gloom felt on the plane and ride over.

We headed down Main Street; the name we gave the widest drag from the last gatehouse. A path, more than anything, it meandered by rusting trailers, equipment rooms, or rotting machines. The list Chicotte handed me had some twenty pieces of equipment needing repair as early as tomorrow. Seeing all the rot out here, a hell of a lot more work would be needed. The brown camo trailed us the whole way.

A creaking came from out of the nightfall. A light came on in a trailer. Someone had been watching us from inside it. A white man stood there smoking a cigar. He puffed, and the smoke coalesced into a kinked balloon above his head. By chance, or coincidence, his face fell in a shaft of darkness. He was the only man we had seen on the walk, maybe the only living being on this side of the property. He waited a hundred feet back.

"Good evening," the man said. He stood like a brilliant trophy, one arm stuck to his side.

He was of average height, thin, with cropped blond hair, and left scrappy at the top in some foppish fashion. He ran his hand through it.

As we approached, the white ink of his form seeped from the dark. We stood near his door, where the outside light now shone like a beacon. Logos stayed far behind me, in the shadow.

"Come closer. Better. I haven't seen a soul in months. Welcome." He took a small step forward but withdrew back up the trailer steps, timid as a child. "I'm Dr. Marc Gardoux, the site geologist, and for the interim, the engineer."

A last name should match an accent. His accent came off more Brit than French, as if it landed south of the Channel, took in the sights, and rowed back across when it got bored.

I introduced myself.

Marc bowed with deliberate, formal manner. He could have been a nobleman, or actor, or the Chaplain Extraordinary on leave from Buckingham Palace. His clothing was another thing all together. Yellow feet poked out of bedroom slippers. A sordid white polo shirt lifted over his navel. His light blue pajama pants were silk.

"Your friend, what about your friend?" he said. "Hello you. What's *his* name?"

Logos's face leaned back beyond the arc of light.

"He's Logos."

Marc's attention was singular, consuming, and could've wrapped its arms around all humanity. He was damned good at it, damned charming, this white trophy in silk knickerbockers. He thought Logos didn't come off very sociable though.

We're tired, the long trip, the bumpy road here, I said. I told him we came from the US.

"Well, fine," he said. "I'm a bit unpolished myself. This place does it." He pointed into the void. "I apologize for my attire."

"We're looking for somewhere to crash."

The full darkness fell over the bush now as a soft duvet. Logos still hadn't said a thing.

Something bothered Marc. He grew impatient, and the nobleman in him took a hike. "Did you bring the mining equipment with you?"

I told him we brought items in crates, all unloaded now. The crates could have held anything, no way of telling. Eight-foot gorillas could have been inside. Mr. K. K. brought us. I pointed back to Logos, telling Marc he was the one going to be repairing it all.

"I see. Well, K. K.? Did he sing? Wretched. How about the drill bits? Did you bring *those*?"

I shrugged.

Marc knotted up his lips, even more prim than before. He became aware of it, loosened the old maw, and a curt smile pointed at us. "Well, three large drill bits expected."

"Three crates," I said.

He grew bolder and came closer. I figured him to be in his late fifties.

I told him about the 8 ft. x 8 ft. spray-painted on all. They barely fit in the fuselage.

Marc looked up to the heavens. "Thank god." His face sat level again, chalky-white even in the shadow.

I wasn't sure if he was even talking to me.

He got himself together. "Friends—my new friends, these are the largest drill bits in the world. Custom-made for the new shaft to be drilled." He became jubilant, the news, his elixir.

"What's so special about them?" Logos asked, out of nowhere.

"He speaks! God has given you a tongue. Still can't see you back there."

Everyone had been waiting for them, he said. They *were* the eight-foot gorillas in the crates, and the keys to unlocking the potential of the

KEM. Made from tungsten carbide, a chemical compound two times tougher than steel, the process sintered them together, compared with conventional steel assembly, and all quite technical. He recited his full resume, and man, did it take a while. He'd been in the profession for, oh, some thirty-odd years, and knew everyone.

It was good to know, I said. But wait, the technology of steel, what about the old yarn? Yes of course. Imagine two ice cubes adhering to one another in a glass of water. The new bond made a stronger surface. What happened to the old bits? Why, everything had been destroyed when they tried to penetrate a deep igneous formation. Really? Yes. Failure—too much failure, he said. They had enough, so we ordered these my boy—these.

"The previous mechanic was removed—no sir, I'm wrong. He absconded."

"What happened to him?" I asked.

"People disappear sometimes, Robert. It's like a gold ring which falls into a street drain. You watch it roll and it disappears—bye. Gone into the hole, never to be seen again. His modifications on the drill bit connection plate didn't work, destroying millions of dollars of drilling equipment. Afterwards, I never saw him again. He rolled into the drain, you could say. Shut down for a year now. Welcome to one of the most disorganized places in the world." He presented the dark void beyond the light. "One country as large as all Western Europe." He took a bow. "A mess."

We told him Chicotte said the shutdown was only a *few* months.

The facts changed in the bush every day, he said. He had to write things down to remember. He filled binders. He advised us, as serious as any grandparent might be on the facts of life, to stay on Chicotte's good side, otherwise, one could end up lodging out here in the snake and rodent wing, permanently. Chicotte's a Master, and Logos and I were soon-to-be Workers. Don't even begin to think it's anything more. Marc handed his broken stick over years ago, and his life had been easier. We should be prepared to do the same.

I suggested, if things were so bad, why didn't he leave and quickly?

He called me, "my boy, my dear boy," again. He had a seven- or eight-digit payday coming when and if they ever drilled Shaft #4. He'd been waiting a decade.

He pushed back the bridge of his spectacles. "I can leave at any time. See?" He showed off his doublewide trailer. "I'm one of the privileged Workers. I make bonuses." He squinted to see Logos in the dark. "Do you know where the word *Chicotte* comes from?"

"No," I said.

He laughed, folded over. "Why, it's the sound the bullwhip made when the Belgians snapped it on these poor souls during colonial times—*chi-cotte!* They made it from sundried Hippo hide cut into sharp corkscrews. His name is a bullwhip sound. Isn't it funny?"

It didn't sound funny.

"When you read about the carnage, it's not. King Leopold of Belgium colonized the Congo Free State and was quite the son of a bitch." He shook his head. "These drill bits, oh, how this village—and the whole bloody region—needs them to work." He tried to pinpoint Logos in the dark. "Mystery man, do you know how to install them?"

No training, or engineering plans came with it, Logos said, but he'd figure it out.

Marc said the drill bits cost millions of dollars. They were as precious as the diamonds themselves, custom-made for the KEM.

Logos assured him he could and would fix anything put before him. It wasn't arrogance, mind you, he said it with all the conviction, integrity, and balls I've ever heard a man muster. Still, I did wonder a bit.

"You're going to take this thing on all by yourself?" Marc said. "Make the world in a day's work? Arrogant, like my father."

Logos said he had something Marc didn't, the tool needed to fix it.

"Ha. What is it?"

"My mind and my reason."

"You *are* the most arrogant man. So, what about the hope of all mankind? Don't they count?"

There's no hoping or wishing, only reason applied to a problem, Logos kept saying.

"Your reason supersedes everything?"

"Yes," Logos admitted.

A cold sweat came over me. I went adrift in uncharted waters, and Logos more than Marc, put us out there, farther, and farther.

"You sir, are delusional," Marc said. Something weighed on Marc's thoughts. "I...have to find a way out of..." He tried to see Logos better. "You sound familiar. Have we ever met?"

"No." Logos motioned for us to get going.

I sensed something off about him from the first moment Marc spoke.

"There is something about you..." Marc said, in a stupor.

"Good night," I said.

I turned back and Marc hadn't moved. He stood there, a trophy on a stand, the light of his trailer covering his quarter. We left him, and the guard followed our every step.

Marc had crossed Logos's path before, somewhere, and I couldn't wait to find out where. At some point, Logos would have to spill the beans about himself and how it got us here.

9
Chile

The trailer Marc described sat out there, on the cusp of the giant hole, lengthwise along the path. We powered it up and dragged ourselves up the steps. The guard stayed watch by the door and lit a cigarette, his face glowing from the ember.

Inside, stale air billowed out as thick as a stew. An ashy pall covered twin beds, nightstands, a plastic foldout table, and ashtray. A settee lay upside down. We flipped the lights and adjusted our eyes. Something odd took up the corner—a curled-up spotted bush snake. A torrent of blood swept through me. White light blinded my thinking. I wanted to kill it. I raised a broom and swung.

Logos's tree trunk arms blocked me, again.

"I don't like snakes," I said.

"They don't like your face, either."

We shined the flashlight on him. Green with black striping, the body kinked and coiled. His black eyes never left us, and when we got too close, the head snapped to one side like a tango dancer. Logos pushed him out.

§

We cleaned up in the brackish water. We ate. We rested. We stared at nothing. We tried eating the "dessert" they offered us earlier, fried grasshoppers. They tasted like old sardines and we spat them out. My stomach wouldn't stop rumbling. My head raced, and I wanted to ask Logos about Marc, but he crashed out. *Wait, Robbie-boy, wait until morning*, I thought. I remembered to assemble facts before asking blustery questions, as Logos had taught me.

Later the old-young noggin went to work, and the slumber gods beckoned. I drifted away.

I kept seeing my parents' faces, all soppy, hanging low, and shaking in surrender because I was leaving for who knew how long. I hated the constant attachment and attention given to me, suffocating my freedom and all. Now, I saw it another way. They were concerned about me and here I was, this self-centered prick, like all the other pricks I had gone to school with, pushing them away. *Idiot.*

I had spoken with my parents before the Town Car picked us up for the airport. They'd already done the bankruptcy dance with their attorneys.

I did the old number punch.

My mom picked up. "The last store closed. We're..." She wept.

I didn't like it. "I'll wire you some money. I have some."

"We love you—wait a minute. Your father said something. What, Honey?"

"Rob," he said in a huff. I could tell he swiped the receiver from her. He always did it, and it pissed her off every time. "Only businessmen count. The rest eats from welfare." He always went off about taxes, and the cold, and the cost of a loaf of bread. It used to cost a quarter in the sixties and look at it now.

"I know," I said, hearing it for the millionth time.

"No one provides like industry. Not the government, *non-monsieur*. So listen and listen well. Dethrone royalty who doesn't produce." His energy poured through the receiver, first time in years. He'd been sick with Influenza A, and this was the old Dad, again.

"Right-o," I said. "Dethrone royalty."

"We'll cope. Here's Mom."

"Bring a jacket," she said.

§

Pounding—someone's pounding at the door. I popped out of bed. For a moment, I thought I still rode my old Huffy in La Fontaine Park. The guard stood there, and Izbart, next to him. Behind them, the sunlight poked through the verticals, and the shafts winded into splinters. It wasn't a dream—we were here, in the shit.

"Mr. Logos, Mr. Robert," Izbart said. "Time for work."

We'd locked the door last night but he had a key.

He turned to Logos. "I wait long time for this day. You get us back to life." He stepped half-way out. "Get ready. I be back, one half hour."

He left, and the guard stayed by the door outside, as I could still see Uncle Kalashnikov's muzzle in the window.

Logos glanced at me. Would he speak? I sensed a man who wanted confession but delayed his walk to the wooden booth.

"Logos isn't your real name," I said. Silence. Surprise. Poker face. Maybe I read him wrong. "Marc couldn't remember it."

He took forever. "It was to protect you." He looked straight ahead the whole time. "Not even these guys know it. It's the way it stays." His head turned back to me. "All right, Marc's part of this Consortium-thing which got us here. Met him years ago in Chile."

"What the fuck? How?"

"It came together last night." He exhaled. "I was on this contract job in Chile, when two men approached me. They said they could change my life. I could spot cheap salesmen about a mile away. I ignored them.

"At the time, I travelled everywhere turning around failed operations. I guess the word got around. I couldn't believe these guys, though. They showed up at my motel at midnight and strutted in as if walking into a nightclub, ready to order drinks. One dressed in a suit, the other, khakis. The khakis stood by the door, the other, next to me. Felt uncomfortable, like being caught in a snatch job, or something. Fuck it, I had a Beretta taped under the bed.

"They wanted to talk business. The South African, Jansen Pretorius, wore a suit. He went on about their organization in Asia, or South America, or somewhere. I guess they wanted to hire me. Who knew? Even claimed I was a foreign agent for a time. The khakis said it. I told him to go to hell. It was Marc from last night. Jansen did most of the talking, though. He wore this black sports coat which shined money. 'I represent a powerful man,' he said. 'He pays me well to see things get done.' I nodded."

I wanted to ask about our predicament, but I let him go on, knowing the answers would come before the questions. The facts trickled in.

They wanted to hire him. They knew his talent, knew of his

deceased wife, his dealings in South America before the mechanic days, as some sketchy agent provocateur. He wouldn't say more about it. When they made him the offer, though, he thought long and hard about it.

"I said no to them. Marc stayed mum, conceited little shit. He kept looking through the window for something, or someone, expecting them to show up at any minute. Jansen continued to press, and I said no, again. They stared at me for a long time, and I thought I was a goner but the phone rang. A silk voice, like some one-eight hundred-hypnotist, asked for Marc. Marc grabbed the receiver, looked at me, and hung up. They walked out to a waiting car. Three years ago."

Nothing in his life was ever the same. He left the company two months later and moved back to Queens to start his own business. His uncle lived there. At the time, Logos had money. He opened a shop and could repair any mechanical device from industrial equipment to the most exotic cars in the world. People found him and paid. In the end, he went broke.

"They red-flagged all my accounts, *persona non grata*," he said. "I couldn't deposit cash in the bank anymore. Someone had to be behind it."

His attorneys couldn't make heads or tails of it. The dominos fell, bills piled up, his power got cut, and employees disappeared. Think about it, every employee disappeared on the same day. Someone had gotten to them and fast. It didn't matter how much he paid them, or his attorneys, or anything. Something seeped into his life, he said, wrapped its fingers around his throat, and squeezed. The bank foreclosed. He was ruined.

"How?" I said. "How did they take you down?"

"I told you."

"I mean, *specifically*, what was it?"

"They control."

"Like a snake?"

"Only bigger, cleverer," he said. "Human boa constrictors which squeeze and kill only when they get the urge."

I said we should make a run for it if we could. If this Consortium could do it to someone there, there's no telling what pain it could inflict on us here.

§

He reminded me of what we saw along the perimeter of the property: bands of spiral barbed wire ran over a ten-foot fence, brown camo sentries stood below like scarecrows. We were in the shit, in the middle of nothing, too far from everything.

"To have a thing," he said, "you must control it first. Control it long enough, you own it. They have us."

"Logos, you're smart. How did they know to control?"

"Knew my weakness, money."

Like poisoning a man's well, they simply waited for him to get thirsty. After a year of this pressure, the Consortium came with a job offer in Peru. Once in a lifetime did a man have a chance to make things right, they said to him. The only problem, they were the ones controlling the opportunity and the life. He'd never heard of them, either. It didn't matter, he needed the money, and the trap had been set, and it became obvious who did it, and why. Few had their unlimited resources, even fewer, clever enough to control the smart.

§

My head swam—the Consortium, the mine, Logos, the barbed wire, Mr. K. K. sitting like an idol on the plane. I once read, pinching your neck hard over the carotid artery and releasing, sent more blood to the brain and pushed the headache out. I pinched it but it didn't work. To hell with it and everything else. What card do we play? How could we get out?

Logos described a fantastic plan—a vision, really. He would push ahead, complete the work they needed him to do and keep us alive. The first part scared me. It would give us time to find an out, impossible as it may seem in the middle of nowhere. The second part blew me away.

"It was their aim?" I said, confirming his idea. "Get you here."

"Extravagant, isn't it?" He looked away, eyes closed as if in prayer. "Extravagant ambition. Meticulous, too." He remembered something. "These people don't make mistakes."

"How is it they don't know your real name?"

When he came from Greece as a child, the birth certificate

name didn't translate well. They called him Logos. It stuck. When he worked overseas, he always used an alias on top of it to avoid kidnap or blackmail. They did it to Western businessmen all the time. Shady characters moved around these mines, always fishing for opportunities.

I asked him straight up if he was involved in the intelligence game, then or now? This could only thrust us upon hot coals, or sharp rocks, depending on his veracity. He laughed it off.

"Well, what's your real name?"

He said he didn't remember, and he would tell me why. "When you give your life to something, and it's taken away, you're destroyed. You'll understand me then."

"We knew the risks before leaving," I said.

He didn't like it. He said we acted on my advice when I read over his employment contract. He trusted me to find the tripwires in the language to keep us out of harm's way and in Midas's good graces and all.

It was bullshit. He knew everything I did, and even got me recruited along. It didn't matter, though, we were here in the same boat, a sinker. And there before me, he drifted away, into himself, where his demons and dogs always roamed.

10

BUILDING MENTAL TOUGHNESS

He was rapt in thought.

"I don't want to talk about it," he said. He was mad at me for landing us here.

So was I, in a way, but I didn't like how he tried to put it all on me, a twenty-one-year-old snotter just graduated and all. I hated the old blame game people did and it got me pissed. White light blinded my thoughts, again. The old wrath and colossus grew in me, and a chasm opened, with the waterfall rushing toward it, demanding to be filled. I controlled it this time by breathing and breathing, to shrink the emotion down to a pebble. The tension fell away. Whew.

At VMA, they taught me to "control my feelings" and all, to quash the anger. When I couldn't control them, they drew the old paddle out and walloped my behind until Satan and his band of brothers were exorcised. I preferred to control the anger on my own, which wasn't often. When I did, I could think. I couldn't do it on demand, yet.

For now, I tried to figure out Logos. Maybe he acted a certain way because I asked about his past, or for the work he would have to do to save our asses, or for having to look out for me; this young, dumb kid who wanted to see it all, be it all before twenty-two. I wasn't sure, but something told me, forget it. Conflicts between real friends are quashed too, in time. Yeah, it's how it is. I shut my mouth and stared outside.

§

Knock. Knock. Izbart craned his head around the open door.
"Ready?" He came in. "You feel well, Mr. Logos?"

"Surviving," Logos said.

It's what everyone was trying to do there, he said. He had some idea of how we were brought here, not the exact way, but he knew how things worked and such. It was the way of the KEM. He and the other Workers had adjusted to the way of life and so would we. For now, we needed to get our rumps in gear, as Chicotte and many "important people" would be at a morning briefing waiting for Logos. The work and our roles would be explained.

We asked for the details.

He wasn't privy, he said, and no one outside Chicotte's little cabal was given information. They simply needed us there, rumps parked in chairs for a few hours, to hear it directly from him. Izbart said they would discuss the machinery needing first aid, operational procedures, the work schedule, the future. He didn't know any more.

"I tell my wife, the man finally here to help the mine. When he help the mine, he help the village."

Of all these guys, I liked Izbart the most, and I think Logos did too. He carried himself with the impeccable manners of a nobility class of gentleman which no longer existed. He was a human being, and whether he knew it, or not, a bright light for two kidnapped blokes.

His mood darkened. "Whole village working in the open pits to get the product out." He reached into his pocket. "My wife send you this from people in village." He pressed an object swaddled in newspaper into Logos's hand. "To guide your hands."

Logos unraveled a small silver cross with a pearly center inlay. He shifted the cross in the faint light, making the pearl glisten. His face remained still. Logos pushed it back into Izbart's hand. "Your own reason is more powerful."

Izbart looked at the floor.

Logos told him the same thing he told me before we left New York: each person was born with reason. They used it as their only means for survival in this world. Applied over and over to complex problems, like layers on a cake, the right solution came. Grasp its reins, and it had the potential to change lives.

Izbart kept on asking him if such a thing could be true. "It free a man from the control of other men?"

"Frees you from psychological bondage, then physical bondage."

Izbart confirmed, "Can a Worker become a Master?"

Logos thought about it. "Reason gives any man the freedom to be neither."

Izbart's question had been answered. He said he would tell his people what Logos said and why. Izbart placed the cross on the chair next to Logos. "Keep anyway, sir."

Bells rang, the same ones we heard on arrival.

"Gentlemen, time to go," Izbart said. He stepped out.

§

I went outside and waited with him. A new guard stood by, smoking and puffing, and puffing and smoking, with his Uncle hung over his shoulder. Izbart stared off into the distance, whistling like a nervous Nellie. I thanked him for warning us yesterday about Chicotte. He nodded and tapped his heart. He paced near an old Land Rover which listed beneath a tree.

We followed Izbart down the path.

Logos's mind continued to work on our situation, never shifting or deviating. Sometimes, I thought I could actually see the cogs and wheels in motion inside. I wondered if he calculated revenge in the machine of his. He told me to keep an eye on Marc and the big man, Chicotte. We couldn't trust them for shit.

"Izbart's people are good," he said. "We can work with them until the time is right." He took in the horizon over the plateau. It shone bright and orange and new. "Until I can get this entire thing running again."

I stopped in my tracks.

He'd said it earlier when he described his "vision" for getting out of here, but I thought it was only talk. This was beyond one man's reach. It blew me away, again. "We should split the first chance we get."

"When I'm good and ready." He confirmed his straight-ahead plan, and it included me along for the ride.

I asked him—begged him to tell me about it.

We would complete the work. Repair of the shiny temple itself is what these guys needed, and it meant they needed him. It meant we stayed alive. So, he would give it to them. This was it, the grand plan for now while we were stuck there. What repairing, or connecting the new headframe entailed, no one would say, yet.

Mr. Logos, what about our out? I thought. *What about keeping our hides in one piece as we tried to get out?* I asked him.

He was working on it, he said, as his attention drifted over the horizon, again.

§

One day while in his office, the same look came over him. He stared at a bizarre clock which hung over my shoulder; a clock made of greasy engine gears. It sat on one of those faux oak boards a trophy shop would use to mount a "Runner Up" figurine for a bake-off or something. It was a real clock, though, accurate and ticking away like any other. It hung alone, as a framed icon on bare space, and a large sprocket gear at the top made the dial face. A metal timing belt ran around it and a smaller gear below. I'll never forget it. Sometimes, I thought a real truck could come crashing through the wall at any moment. He always looked at it, too, but it wasn't for the time of day—no. He ached for the time he had somehow lost because of the clock itself. I've seen such a look once or twice in my life. It is a haunted empty gaze which only deep pain can bring about. The same look came over him.

11

He snapped back to his old self. I imagined some invisible tether connected him to the clock, which could release him at will. He brightened, and the world seemed new again. He claimed—no demanded—his achievement here would make history on the continent. It sounded like revenge to me.

Izbart turned around. "Gentlemen, we meet in there for the briefing."

He pointed to a perfect cube of concrete before us. A thick antenna projected out from the center, nearly scraping the pink-orange clouds running above. He went inside.

I hoped for a signal from Logos, something telling me he came to his senses, or at least changed his mind. I told Logos I was scared.

He told me to think about something. "They engineered this soiree. They know only one man's capable of completing the job—me. So, they won't harm us, yet."

I reminded him of what Marc said about the previous mechanic. "He's dead. Gone. Were chickens in a coop."

Sure, but without Logos, this thing would become their greatest failure. He told me to picture a new Rolls Royce, window sticker still on, sitting in the bush, which no one could drive. He held the keys.

I became drowsy. I knew my face showed it.

"Wake the hell up," he shouted.

"I will—I am."

He wasn't convinced. When it came to fear, he said, we should think of the cornered snake from last night. The snake didn't have any

options, either. It said, "I'll fight you to the end, you bastards. Come
on!" In the moment, the snake felt alive. Why? He placed his life as
the highest value. He would fight to keep it, and it was a valiant act. It
sounded good coming from Logos but didn't help explain my fear.

He pressed his index finger against my cheek like a dagger. "Do
you want to die?"

"*No.*"

"We are slaves. We will do what we need to do. Got it?"

It needed to be said, again. I knew it all along, but deflected, or
suspended the belief, or ran from it like the half men we became on the
plane. He'd said it before, only another way: deflection evaded reality—
it's a lie. I couldn't lie to myself anymore about anything.

This was our reality. I knew it, felt it, but couldn't admit it happened
to two white guys. Things like this, or on the news, or overheard at
a coffee shop, happened to someone else, somewhere else, while we
stayed all comfy in our beds, or cubicles, or coffee shops *watching* it
happen to someone else. But we were like them, normal people, sort
of, who ended up in the wrong spot with the wrong pricks pulling the
strings, and the whole time we felt special, in a different class from the
others, even though we walked around behind the same barbed wire as
them. No, we were flesh and blood, and so were they. The mirage faded.

§

Logos shifted his eyes to the highest point below the mountaintop.
The shiny black temple came next. It drew him, cradled his senses,
and he hated himself for not knowing why. His reason, or some other
inexplicable force, thrust him back to the here and now.

"You're afraid," he said. "So am I. We hold our lives in our hands.
From here on, we play with nothing to lose."

He dissected fear like a surgeon, and to this day, I've never heard
anyone describe something so complicated in an easy-peasy way. The
smartest people can always describe complex things in their simplest
form, and for a moment, we feel as smart as them. He explained, fear
ran through us as an impulse. We understood it as an emotion, as the
sensation of imminent vulnerability. We recognized it in our brain's
amygdala *first*, and it ran into the body as an emotion *later*.

It's funny. I always thought it was the other way around.

When it's present, he said, we couldn't think rationally. Knowing it had a kind of *predictability*, brought us a step closer to fully understanding it. I mean, it wasn't a spirit, or ghost, or a mist, but something in us, originating in the old noggin.

Wow, I was alive again. It diffused the cloud of this thing we were under. I say *thing*, since it describes something I wasn't sure how to define. I sensed it as a weight overhead which never fell, only hovered with intent. It stayed put, true, and on us.

"I'll complete the work," he said. "If I don't, we're vulnerable. Eliminate the vulnerability, reduce the fear. I've been reading the book."

§

Before we left New York, David had given him a simple black book, ascetic as a bible, *Building Mental Toughness*. It happened in the Consortium's office in Pennsylvania, days before the Lincoln dropped us off at the airstrip. Potentials under contract with the organization and heading overseas to the most remote regions of the world, were given it.

"Think of it as a vaccine," David had said.

Red soil stained it all the way through to the title. It was dusty, too, like a relic unburied from the depths of Mars. David had the balls to say only one copy existed in the world. It killed me, man.

Logos scoffed, pushed it back across the desk with his middle finger to him.

"I'm not asking," David said. "Take it. It's the *only* vaccine for the mind." He returned it across the desk with his middle finger. "You'll thank me."

The book teetered on the edge, fell, but Logos caught it.

David leaned back into his chair for the first time. He was a cold bastard who stared at nothing. He's the one guy I met in my life whom I could never figure out.

§

We stood in front of the white cube building. I turned the knob to who knows what. Logos reminded me, whatever happened inside the room, we played with nothing to lose. He also reminded me, I had said

I wanted to make history. I said it when we first met, and it seemed like a long time ago, now.

"We'll make history," he said.

I nodded vague understanding, not sure if he meant I would make history, or he.

I opened the door. The sunlight behind us flash-banged the innards of a cave.

12
THE KING

Noxious fumes made it hard to walk, much less breathe. The room lay covered under licks of beige paint, still wet, and dripping. In the corner, Mr. K. K. sat on his haunches, rifle between his legs. He scanned each passerby, his eyes, heavy, flat, dark.

Despite the heat, idle fans with new tags lay cocooned in cellophane. Guards in blue or brown camos stood like wilting bronzes. Men in hardhats sat apart from everyone else, sweating too. I never saw them without their helmets. It was part of their skin, who they were. They were Workers who held rank over the T-shirted men but not over the camos. The Masters had masters, too, and the blue camos held rank over the brown camos in the hierarchy.

Chicotte held court behind a podium. He dressed in his Sunday's best: green military cottons, shoulder straps, beret, and bronze medals. They said he made it to the rank of colonel in the DRC army, but who knew. Several Congolese men in white button-down shirts stood by fielding his jokes. A voluptuous Congolese woman in a dashiki drew their attention. She wrote on a small pad. It wasn't anything about his stand-up, I thought, but something about each person in the room. Perspiration beaded on her neck and over her looped earrings.

Bits of conversations jumped between the groups, hushed, and re-connected like railcars in the dense air. When we entered, the chatter ended.

Marc sat near the podium. His pompous grin beamed. "How are tricks, gentlemen?"

Neither one of us was in the mood for this kind of crap, especially after the talk we had outside.

"So, *Lo-gos*—if that's your real name. Remember Chile?"

Logos didn't buy anything this guy had to sell, ever again. He told Luc anyone living in the snake and rodent wing's been demoted.

Marc raised his nose. "Soon this plot of land will be the most valuable dirt in all Africa." His index finger spun a taut lasso.

"I'll create it, you'll watch," Logos said.

Although restrained most times, a revengeful streak beat below Logos's chest. It became evident in drips and drops. It worried me.

Chicotte approached with the court. Several scruffy beards dressed in colorful dashikis joined them; the elders, we presumed. A tall dashiki man, in matching orange kofia cap, stood in the middle. He held on to a cane, and thick-framed glasses magnified his black eyes.

The voluptuous woman stayed glued to him. She acted as his eyes and ears, always aware of the other men around him. When she saw a chance, she wrote on her pad, again.

"Surprised the night we visited?" Marc said. "Scared, more accurate?"

The court listened.

Logos gave the old poker face. He said, if two men show up on your doorstep at midnight, either someone you know died, or it's you who's about to.

Marc pleaded his case. He had a job to do at the time, he said, nothing else, really, truly. He wouldn't say on who's instructions, or anything. He smirked and crossed one knee over the other like some country gentlemen watching a polo match. I once saw a magazine ad where a guy did the same thing. At the time, I thought it looked refined, now, not so much.

Marc wanted to kiss and make up. He called himself the best damned geologist in Africa. "The best."

"Geologist or prospector?" Logos said.

"I've broadened my horizons."

No matter how many times Marc thrust his head back, or clicked his folded leg, or clucked his tongue, Logos saw past it and knew his aim. He had told me veterans in backwater mining operations eked out a living by the skim, the pass along, the commission transported in body cavities, which made a bonus check.

"I have the equity I always deserved, *Lo-gos*. I'm fine. Fine really."

"Zilch. You *appropriate* when no one's looking."

"Don't cross the line, young man! You may not come back."

Everyone looked over now.

"A threat?"

Marc noticed them. "Of course not." He backpedaled, forgive, and forget, and he curled a comma smile for all in the room to see. "Who cares? We got you here as planned."

Logos readied for launch. His right hand clasped the back of the left, making a "v" of his hanging arms. He told Marc, as head field technician, he held the cards, and to guess which ones.

"Go straight to Hell," Marc said.

"I'm already here."

Logos became this cold bastard like David, and I couldn't read him, either. He worried me even more.

"You like reasoning, Marc?"

"Ha. I don't like *mental magic*."

"If a mine has great wealth, and mechanical talent is necessary to extract the wealth, talent can create wealth. *Magic*."

The man with the cane mouthed "mental magic" to Chicotte. The man leaned on his cane, bowing it, scratching the beige floor. Fashioned from a tree branch, human hands must've smoothed and lacquered it a thousand times over.

The court weighed what they heard. They pointed, nodded, whispered "magic, control mind" to each other. It wasn't good.

Izbart stood in the back of the room listening.

"You corrupt the mind," Chicotte said to Logos. He said it as if someone had insulted him personally.

Mr. K. K. stepped near Chicotte, and his gaze shifted my way.

Logos took in the faces of the semicircle. He clarified his statement as a logical argument, nothing more. He was scared, too.

A giant guard, the size of a football player, raised his hand to speak. It was a blunder. He knew it and dropped it in a second. His lips quivered. "C...common sense, sir."

"I slap you down," Chicotte said.

He grabbed the guard by the throat, and the young man's eyes bulged from their sockets. He shook him like a ragdoll, even though the guard was the same size as him. It was quite a feat. The guard apologized, but it didn't matter. Chicotte threw him like a wiffleball into the foldout chairs, and into the men in hardhats, which tumbled, too. Brown camo guards surrounded him, and no one dared help. He moaned.

Chicotte pivoted back to Logos. "Stop this ungodly thinking."

The man with the kofia cap sighted his cane at Logos. "This man can incite a riot in the village." His breathing quickened, head tilted, body contracted, the cane sighted straight out at Logos. "Chicotte, you keep his mouth closed."

Logos didn't understand and neither did I. What did this man think Logos would tell those out there in the field? The mine was a failure? Their old temple, crumbled? Their new one, dead on the operating table for lack of a proper surgeon?

"No talk like this in front of King Ulindi," Chicotte said. He pointed to the man with the cane and everyone bowed. "He represents Kivu. The whole giant territory. Everything the people have been taught to believe. Apologize."

Things needed to be kept simple, the king said. Men will be confused with this talk. They should think of their brothers, their neighbors, and what they needed, *first*. There needed to be leadership. This collective ruled the mine and he ruled the collective. Got it?

"They have a responsibility to themselves, *first*," Logos said. "For their own lives."

"You insult my people," the king said.

I looked at Logos, thinking the same. Why all this? Let's do what we came here to do and get the hell out. I remember what he had said: he knew they needed him—only him to complete this project and breathe new life into the territory. At this point, he still had some leverage, impunity cost nothing, but could end up costing us everything.

King Ulindi looked at each person in the face. He said men worked when they told them, for how much, and where. The KEM collective was the brain, the men, its body.

"Every man has reason and the right to use it," Logos said.

The king didn't care for Western talk, he said. Workers needed money. Mothers needed to make milk. Everyone needed to take care of their village, simple as one, two, three.

Chicotte brushed by us, reeking of mouthwash and liquor. He pressed his forefinger against his temple. "You say to confuse the simple minds here," he said to Logos. Chicotte's eyes blurred and the pupils dilated. Fragments shifted in the dark saucers.

I saw the cold gaze of a blackbird. It stirred the fear in me. I experienced the same thing on the plane, during the ride into the bush, and when Logos called us slaves. This time, I stared at the floor for some reason. I tried to get a grip, blinked, refocused, and when I looked back, the image disappeared. I was shaken. Why?

The voluptuous woman whispered to the king.

He stepped closer and rammed his cane into the floor. "I hold you responsible for the future failure of this mine." Dead quiet, and it became hard to breathe.

"Sir, how will the mine fail when it's *already* failed?" Logos said. "The mine failed before I ever got here. I'm here to correct the problem."

The eyes and jaws of the court fell open.

King Ulindi peered sideways at Logos. "If the Workers do not trust your words, the mine will fail."

Logos shook his head.

Oh god, here it comes.

"King, the sequence doesn't make sense. If I step onto wet ground, it doesn't mean I threw water on it. If I step onto a failed mine, I didn't make it fail. It's a false cause."

Guards and button-downs nodded to each other, agreeing with the easy as pie common sense. Maybe they read it on a kitchen apron too.

It made sense, but who gives a shit. He said it because he could. A stratagem, perhaps? Maybe he needed to put these pricks on their heels momentarily. Maybe an inch of power sufficed to keep us respected, and if respected, maybe still alive. I hoped I was right.

The king talked to each man, while the voluptuous woman made notes. She served as some all-in-one paralegal, secretary, and advisor.

Mr. K. K. stepped up, rifle over his shoulder.

Two button-downs spoke with the king and Chicotte, and judging from their smiles, their last-minute entreaties saved the orbit of the planet from deviating.

Chicotte took the podium. "Friends, good workers, we must forget these baby-small issues. The mine is life. The mine must produce. We have the will to make it produce a new life, and we have the man now to do it. Let's move to next stage in production. Agree?" He pressed his head forward seeking the nod from the KEM collective, and above all, the king with a cane.

King Ulindi and the court nodded their satisfaction. He pushed the door open with his cane and out they went. The light from the door flash-banged when it opened. As the king and court went out, a guard pushed a bare-chested man through the jamb, holding him there. The old wise man in purple pants who insulted Mr. K. K. yesterday, struggled to free himself. Mr. K. K. came up and slapped him across the face and they took him away.

A shrill cry came from outside.

Izbart came over to the window to see. A camo told him to go away. Izbart obeyed. Although a high-ranked Worker, Izbart knew his place before the camo Masters.

The giant guard Chicotte threw across the room, moaned back to life. He tried to stand but slipped and came crashing back down. Six camos lifted him clean off the floor, three on each side and ran toward the front door with his head set as a battering ram—boom. No way he survived.

13

Briefing

The big egos with their big words, calmed down, or left, and it felt a hell of a lot better without them. Like watching a leaky football flop over in a garage, a gradual decompression occurred inside the beige room, too. Except for Marc, and Chicotte, the other pricks left with the big prick, the king, and the court. About a dozen of us remained, including Izbart, the hardhats, several camos, and the creeping shadow, Mr. K. K., who returned. When I felt like being watched, I'd look around, and there he was, looking and creeping, creeping, and looking.

We didn't know what happened to the guard or to the man in the purple pants. When we asked someone, they would look away or shush us.

Marc took up his old seat in the rows of chairs.

"Most entertainment I've had in years," he said from across the room. He interlocked his fingers behind his head, overjoyed at the grilling Logos got. "I thank you!" He shrugged and giggled. "I guess they don't like this sort of mumbo jumbo and all. You know..."

"I understood it," I yelled back.

"Like I said, don't get on their bad side." He shook his head, made an invisible noose, and hung himself. "You two have hell later today." He pursed his lips at the podium, where Chicotte read over something. "Listen, learn."

The paint fumes and heat made me nauseous. Maybe what Logos put us through is what did it. I guess he was a certain way. But look, nothing happened; we were still here, plugging along, dizzy, morose from the heat. Someone recommended we drink water. We both drank a gallon and felt better. What medicine. Water served as the cure-all for any ailment in Africa. Got a headache? Drink more water. Arthritis? Drink more water. Snake bite? Drink more water. Too short, can't get it up? Drink more...

Everyone was baking inside the room, and no one would do a damned thing about it. The only air came from an old ceiling fan, with caned blades shaped like leaves, which made long squeaking orbits. Oddly, it's the only mechanical piece which worked.

We parked our rumps on the other side of the room, near four hardhats. They ran the conveyer belts, and the old, and new headframes. In the old-timey days, when things functioned, they plied the subterranean labyrinth where the drill rod pierced the depths.

Chicotte took his time at the podium. While he got his act together, we ate, read several technical documents, and drank more water. My book paid off, as I could decipher the names of parts located underground, or on the mining topography. In general, I understood what went where, but not much beyond. For the office-raised, non-mechanical types like me, it posed a hurdle.

Logos reviewed it all in parallel: the book David gave him, my book, his notes, my notes, and his drawings. He had begun another drawing; an object which looked like a flying saucer, only smaller, and labeled, "Twister Plate." From the looks of it, something would be connected to it, and the whole thing would be re-connected into the drill rod. He rolled up all the renderings, put them in his rucksack, and carried them around like some architecture or archeology student going to class. It reminded me of Indiana Jones, when he held all the rolled-up maps as a professor at his university.

Sometimes, when Logos thought no one watched him, he looked out the window, or at nothing, simply lost in thought. I never saw him once—not a single time—devote himself to anything personal. He never mentioned his family, looked at a picture, or told a story of how he may've gotten wasted at a party, hooked up with a girl, and at sunrise, got arrested for doing something dumber than dumb—no, nothing, nil. His personal life had the antiseptic quality of a laboratory. He held the key to it, too.

§

The hardhats glanced back at us. They were all Congolese men who lived in the village. At times, it felt odd to be the only white men in the room. Except for Marc, we were the only white men around. As the thought came, it left, and I sensed a receptive tone from our soon-to-be friends. Their faces were bright and eager to speak. One looked at Logos and said hello.

"The man with the master plan?" the younger looking of the two said. He clicked his head back. "Know how to attach drill bit to twister plate?" He made abroad smile. "It is not easy."

"I know," Logos said.

We confirmed the drill bit/twister plate attachment as the "special installation" Chicotte mentioned. Marc mentioned it last night, but we couldn't trust a damn thing coming out of his mouth anymore. I had a feeling Logos suspected this type of connection, from his new drawing and all.

"The last mechanic, he disappear," the young man said. He cupped his hand around his ear. "Tell me, sir. How will you do this?"

Logos looked up to the ceiling, teasing. "*Very* carefully."

The men laughed and we shook all around. A row of guards watched us.

The younger man's hardhat kept falling over his eyes, and he tipped the brim back. "I am Jando. This my colleague-friend, Erik." Erik had a moustache.

Chicotte readied his speech. Jando and Erik spun back around.

Mr. K. K. handed Chicotte something to read. He read it, crumbled it into a ball, and flung it against a wall. The wrestler stormed out. Mr. K. K. followed him but stopped at the door, looked our way, and decided to stay. Later, he walked aimlessly about the cube.

Erik turned back around to Logos. "They talk about what you can do."

"Good or bad?" Logos said.

"Only things."

Erik explained their customs. When they met someone new, they riddled them with a series of questions. Part hazing, part curiosity, it became all gameshow entertainment for the interrogators, watching them in the hotseat. The person answering had to sit there and take it. It became a fun way to learn about someone.

Jando kept elbowing Erik, prodding him to ask a question. Jando could hardly contain himself and elbowed some more.

"Be cool, my man," Erik said. He cleared his throat. "So, Mr. Logos, if everything is visible, what is it which cannot be seen?"

"It's not a, 'Nice to meet you,' kind of question, now is it?"

"No, but it say, 'Let us skip small talk.'"

Logos thought about it. "What cannot be seen? God, or another dimension, if either exists."

The youngsters became wide-eyed.

Erik said, "Right, right!" about a dozen times. He shot a look to Jando.

Jando looked ready to burst. He slurped from two cups of coffee, and his legs bounced up and down like pistons. He had a long thin face in the shape of an almond, and when his hardhat fell over his eyes, it made him look like a boy. He urged us to scoot in.

Erik told him to speed up.

"Mr. Robert, you listening?" Jando said. A mischievous squint rolled in his eye. "So, three must cross a river. The first one looks, crosses it. The second one looks but does not cross alone. The third one never sees the river and does not cross it by their own power. Who are these?"

I shrugged from the get-go.

Logos knew. The first one is a woman, he said. The one, who saw the river but did not cross it alone, is the child the woman carries on her shoulders.

Yes, correct, I can't believe it, the boys said. They grew wide-eyed, again.

"And the third?" Jando said. "What about the third?" He nudged Erik.

Logos thought for a moment. "The one who never sees the river is the baby the woman carries in her womb."

"Holy crappity-crap," I said.

"Excellent," Erik said. "Mr. Logos, excellent." He pushed Jando, and Jando pushed him back.

§

We got to talking, and they asked how we got there. Logos clammed up, as he preferred it to lying. I told them there was a mix-up in personnel, and instead of Peru, they dropped us at this inhospitable doorstep. I didn't like lying about it but what was the point? We were here behind the barbed wire for now, and no one was getting out anytime soon.

They didn't buy it.

So, I told them what actually happened. Man, their jaws hardly dropped open. They'd heard of these kinds of things happening at other mines, and it happened at the KEM before, too. It wasn't the first time two white guys, or two black guys, or an entire village had been kidnapped and sent to one of these camps.

I asked him to tell us more, especially about them, and the village, and how it all worked. Were they prisoners, too? Jando wanted to say something but dropped it all when the creeping shadow appeared behind us.

Mr. K. K. had heard everything. His wooden smile pushed his scars outward; holes, lines, mountain ranges, a hamburger of flesh made taut. "You boys have fun time?" The eyes, dead, nothing but ornaments.

Everyone whispered so he could leave.

Mr. K. K. put the rifle barrel to his lips like a finger. "Shh." He stepped closer. "You, Mr. Logos. You like the quiz-gameshow?"

No one would speak.

"My father say, why is man like a pepper? Until you have tested him, you cannot tell how strong he is." He told me to remember it, too.

He still held a grudge from the scrap on the plane. He was the type.

I've known plenty of them before. I dealt with these kinds of pricks at VMA, in Montreal. I busted a nose or two open to keep the bully parasites in check. I didn't want to—I had to. It was them or me, see? At the time, I didn't care about the old rage boiling in me, and who got hurt, and what it would cost. It worked there, trust me. Except for the time these bunch of pricks grabbed me and locked me in the locker room overnight. I was always scared of being taken away—kidnapped—and held in the dark, ever since I was a kid. I got it, though. When they slammed the door shut, and I knew no one was coming back, I caterwauled all night. The pricks laughed but I got through it. I learned to manage, to even control the old wrath at times. But here, with all the barbed wire and stuff, and Uncle Kalashnikov around, I took a different approach. I kept my mouth shut and my jab down.

§

Erik laughed at Mr. K. K. It didn't seem like a good idea, as it spread like a dirty joke in a classroom. Jando and Erik nearly bawled. It kept growing, funnier because of the audience.

Mr. K. K. didn't like it. "You laugh at a Master?"

"No Master, sorry." Erik straightened his face. Upon hearing "Master," he and Jando looked down.

Mr. K. K. tapped his temple. "I will remember you."

His gaze cut through Erik; a look so wicked it sent shivers through us. The old man put the rifle barrel to his lips, again, and walked away. We all looked at each other.

Erik told me an odd story about Mr. K. K. The old man kept a shelter for wounded animals on the property and looked after them like some doting father. Whenever one would get lost, or hurt, Mr. K. K. was there to help. It ran in the family, as his father was a traveling village vet for a time. It made me see a man, despite being a prick, could have a good side, too. He assured me some Masters did have a good side. It was hard to imagine, though, especially when it came to the old man.

§

Chicotte came back to the podium. He cleared his throat and focused with a nervous formality, as if he were about to speak to millions from a stage. Somewhere over our heads floated the imaginary movie camera he made love to, and he looked there more than at us. He made eye contact with us occasionally but wouldn't hold it with any one person. He wiped the sweat from his forehead, took dramatic pause, and went on to say four billion dollars had been extracted over the past twenty years from the old hole. Working with "The Mr. David," marked the instrumental relationship for his success and for everyone else's. He went through a history of the mine, his expertise, his tight bond with the king, reaching rank of colonel in the army, his marriage, four kids, love of cricket and soccer, mine rules and regs, details of the property, our boundless prospects, equipment and its location, tools available, who to talk to for what, who not to talk to, and the timetable for the installation of Shaft #4.

He told us about his childhood. He had run away from home as a tike, and the Belgian Army took him in to do the soldier's laundry, wash their tin cups, and cook up stew. He didn't have anything or anyone else to rely on. He loved them, and they loved him, and became his family. His military career had begun. He went on, all sobby and Homeric.

He mentioned the barbed wire fence, and how the watchtowers, with armed men, stood by waiting for "opportunities." He let it sink in. He outlined the labor hierarchy: blue camos were at the top, t-shirted men, at the bottom. Workers could never become Masters, but Masters could become Workers. It's the way it had been in colonial times, and they kept to those traditions. If someone didn't know the tradition, or their rank, they would find out in time.

He raised his finger. An important news flash: alcohol wasn't permitted on the property but understood by all, thirst conquers commandment. Masters were not allowed to drink the poison, but Workers, as their only escape vice, were allowed two drinks per month on a certain day. Man cannot live by water alone. He stepped away, waving to the crowd.

We exchanged glances with Jando and Erik, and they said they would see us later.

Izbart motioned for us to meet him outside.

I could tell something raged inside of Logos; he hadn't said a goddamn thing. I'd had plenty of experience reading something similar on my face in the mirror.

"You okay, man?" I said.

He looked gone. "These fuckers have us under the boot," Logos said to himself. "If it's how it is, it's how it is." He stood and looked around. "They'll watch me make history here."

I couldn't be sure if he spoke to me or not, but I knew the history would be his. He didn't look at me until we were outside again.

14
THE DRUDGE

The noon light bleached the view up to the hills; trailers, shrubs, and new A-frame, all bleding their colors. Tree and plant life stood still, and the air had built-up into a thick stew. The mercy of a breeze or shadow impossible.

We sweat on our way to Chicotte's office to see Izbart.

"You believe those witch doctors?" Logos said.

"More witch than doctor."

He smirked.

"Insulting the king?" I said. "You're going to get us killed."

"I got them exactly where I want them."

"Where?"

He stopped. "In a headlock. You watch my back."

In the distance, a caterwauling rose over the plateau. It pitched and softened like an eerie chant. One kind recognizes itself in another, and it reminded me of my own cry when I found myself chained on the plane, and years before, when they locked me in the VMA locker room overnight. The cries came from near the old wooden headframe. An object hung some twenty feet off the ground, pinned to its side, wrenching to free itself of a trap. Two men in a jeep shadowed us as we got closer.

We knew the shape of the object, but the mind always takes time to register a foreign object set in a familiar spot. A man hung from shackles halfway up, his legs strapped down by heavy rope. Tic-tac-toes had been sliced into his face, and the blood dripped in dark splotches. A guard stopped us from getting any closer but we didn't need to. The young brown camo which stood up to Chicotte had been nearly crucified on the wood frame. They stripped him bare for all to see. A black bird sat near his shoulder, choking on the dust. The man choked too and cried. This giant of a man cried. I thought someone passing by might come to help him at any moment, but no one did. It turned my stomach.

What could we do, really? We were in a different place, and it worked like no other. Back at home, someone would call the police, but there were no phones here, no police, no lawyers to file a goddamn complaint, or anything. That was the old world; this was the new. It reminded me, someone could disappear off the face of the Earth out here and never be heard from again. We had to keep moving.

We asked the guards what in the hell was going on, but their rifle butts told us to move. Approaching Chicotte's office, Logos didn't mention anything about what we saw, and I kept my mouth shut, too. It burned me up inside.

Logos asked me to brief him. He wanted to know, specifically, the work which waited for him. Since I had the list, I told him the generators and electrical would be done first, the headframe, last. The preliminary list had twenty pieces of equipment.

"More coming," I said.

In *Core Drilling*, they talked about the four pillars of industry: drilling, excavation, sorting, and transportation. In our case, all needed repairs.

Logos looked back at the guard tied to the headframe. He turned to me, and his face hardened. "You ready to make history?"

He was pissed about what happened earlier in the room, or to the guard, or heat, or the fact this shady group of guys who tried to recruit him years ago, snatched him, and threw him into the lion's den. It occurred to me, the last part is what got him. Until he could put them in a real headlock, or exact the kind of revenge he planned for, he would remain this way.

"Yeah, I'm ready," I said.

§

Inside Chicotte's office, Izbart held a stack of paper. "Gentlemen, here is the complete list." He handed it to me.

The list could've been a thin accordion but without keys or buttons to play. The weight promised back-breaking work for its drudge.

I passed it on to Logos, and he flicked through it like a flipbook. One page described a Terex Titan dump truck, sixty-seven feet by twenty-two feet, and three stories high. I couldn't believe it. The twelve-foot tires cost two hundred and fifty thousand—each. Holy—

"What do you think?" Logos said.

"You're the one," I said.

"Let's go."

"Done."

Izbart came around from a table. He wanted to talk.

Logos could be a moody SOB, especially today. In his mind, he was already out there battling the elements, dinosaurs, and rot. When he fell into his rut, no one—I mean no one could get him out of it and convince him the sky was still blue.

Izbart wouldn't be denied. "Mr. Logos, sir, I never hear someone talk like you to our king, or Chicotte." His words came measured, as anything he said could be construed as being disloyal to the KEM collective. He stuck to protocol, the tradition of Master-Worker, and to honor, as would befit a proper gentleman. "This change my life."

Logos stayed distant.

"What you say—my god. It move me, sir." He wanted—needed to risk something. He pointed toward the village. "You say what we only think."

Logos sparked a kind of revelation in people, and they came out and said all kinds of fascinating things about themselves. They trusted him like a wise granny who has heard it all, been it all, and wouldn't judge. I imagined him wearing the kitchen apron will all the proverbs in cursive. It killed me every time.

Logos may as well have been on Pluto.

"Forgive me," Izbart said. "You are deep in thought. I will tell my people what you say. They will understand."

We walked away.

I had to know what was happening to everyone speaking out. I turned around. "The man in purple pants?"

Izbart's gaze shifted down. "We call him the Black Socrates." He came closer. "He gone, sir. Here we have one way—the way of Chicotte. He is the *mayor* in La Petite Ville. When someone no follow, they go bye-bye."

Mr. K. K. approached from the white cube.

My eyes pointed at him. "Is he the *vice mayor*?"

Izbart bit his bottom lip. "Police captain. *Comprendre*?"

"Yes."

"Gentlemen, the work begins. Good luck."

The open jeep from earlier skid to a stop in front of us. The guards motioned for us to get in the back. They were like the other camos: snotty, blank faces, and focused on the job ahead. They were in a shitty mood, most times, but they were Masters.

All guards were considered Masters and their glares confirmed it. It confirmed a superiority ingrained in them since Masters were anointed with the power to supervise Workers. Their eyes always searched us for something. Chicotte had said it was normal. For the Workers always had weaknesses which made them weak, and the Masters had strengths which made them strong.

There were naturally strong men, weak men, smart men, clever men, and dumb men. When the Masters spotted the weak, or dumb, or too smart, or clever, they stomped out their dumbness, or weakness, or cleverness, and created new men, productive men, obedient men, quiet men, and made a better Worker. He'd described the process as ironing a wrinkled shirt. The men were the wrinkles, and the heat and weight of the iron in the hand of a Master would flatten them and make them part of the neat efficient whole. We hadn't officially surrendered as Workers, yet. If we did, we'd eventually be allowed lighter work, and breaks, and so forth. We were newbies about to be ironed, and it's what these pricks were waiting for.

§

We got in the jeep. A blue camo drove, and a brown camo sat in the passenger seat, both smoking their darts for lunch. The brown camo drew in deep, held, and relinquished a puff which turned into a flying boa. He placed a handheld radio on the dashboard. The blue camo man told him to hold it, and they argued about it for a minute. The radio still sat on the dashboard. We were about to see the rest of the mine in the full light of day.

We drove, and the scent of animal musk hung in the air. There were signs about them everywhere: "Warning. Wild Animals. Do Not Walk

Outside of Protective Fence." A flurry of bullets turned this one into a giant cheese grater. The dinosaurs came around; big yellow tractors decomposing into fossils. Rust ate the shell like disease.

The mist hung like a veil in the high hills. Where it fell, it soaked the rocks black. My head felt the old fuzziness each time I looked at the mist. I didn't understand why. The other side of the mine came around.

A curving road, a hairpin, a cliff on my side, sheered straight down. Large rocks clung to the edge, and zephyrs carried the falling mist over the cliff. On the horizon, trees baked, water scattered silver light. The jeep rolled in the hairpins, and no rails protected the shoulders. This wasn't the kind of place safety meant anything. There were no seats or belts to save us boys in the back, either. A metallic grinding came from beneath the floorboard.

"The differential's off," Logos said, looking down. "Bad bearings."

I shrugged.

§

Even way out here, T-shirted men sat on rotting contraptions with no particular aim. They stared at the ground, or blue sky, or the rusting dinosaurs in the graveyard. What were they doing? What were they waiting for? When they stood, their wet skin became glass in the sun. We kept on through the stew, breathing in the game.

A pair of buildings sat over a knoll. We were on it, high, and it dropped down. We had to cling to the roll cage or be tossed. The jeep slammed into a rusty puddle, and the handheld radio flew out. Murky water rained down as a dirty shower, making the camos's darts smolder. We stopped for the brown camo to retrieve his radio. The blue camo got pissed, but no one said a damned thing.

Ahead, the border fence ran behind a building tilting in the silt. Red dust clung halfway along the length of the building, fading as it climbed. Barred windows cut out along the width, and a thick antenna poked out, tethered to four ground stakes.

"Radio room or jail?" Logos murmured.

It looked like the briefing room's dark twin. If it was a jail, it was long ago, as the brush reclaimed it, pulling it into its breast more each day.

On the other side of the road, a CBS block structure led into the trees. The blue camo guard unlocked the door. He flicked the lights up and down a few times until a warehouse with putrid stagnant water flicked on. Anyone could've been electrocuted, as the room brimmed with generators, but they were all dead. There were all sizes: small, long, fat, most with big feet for foundations.

"Tools there," the blue camo man said.

I could tell he was a real prick. Everything out of his mouth said, this was far below his pay grade, and we weren't worth his timesheet and all. That kind of contemptuous crap. He pointed to a large red toolbox, again. "*Your* tools. Go to work." Rusty wrenches, wires, and screwdrivers protruded from the drawers.

Logos went at it. He pulled at each drawer, rattling off the tool inventory to me. He looked into the guts of the generators. Dust and flies and dead rats made their beds. Logos barely noticed and ripped through the machines as if they were made of papier-mâché. Nothing could stop him. I even forgot I was watching a mechanic at work, as his focus reminded me of a veteran surgeon in the operating room performing life-saving surgery. He kept on, and the work kept on, and the heat made it all impossible.

The blue camo's radio screeched. "All okay. Going good," he said. For some reason, he held it upside-down to talk.

Logos pounded away, obsessed with completing the generators in days not weeks. He would say, "Robert, get me this," or "No, wrong! Listen to me. Get me that."

I busted my hump and did what he said.

§

The camos had their own thing going on. The blue camo was a vane bastard, especially about his fingernails. He kept them clean throughout the day—fastidious really, as if some hot date waited for him later. He put the old pincers under the light to pick the crap out from under the bad ones. It's what he did all day, until a funny cat-and-mouse game ensued. Each time the blue looked up from his manicure, the brown feigned a cough but actually ate some nuts. When the blue fidgeted with his nails, the brown chucked a nut—smack, and it hit him in the face. The blue glared back, and the brown got busy working.

Holy crap it was hot. It ground the work slower with every movement, but we did what we needed to do. We did what they said.

They said it with contempt, always, so I hated these pricks, and this place, and how it made you feel like less than something, less than a full man. Man, I wanted to get the hell out of there.

§

A few years ago, I bought a paperback at a supermarket checkout with my change. It was about a prison break, and these two genius criminals who refused to do their time in a Louisiana maximum security block. As you can imagine, they were planning an escape from the get-go. They hated these prick guards, the routine, taking orders, and occasionally ending up in the hole. It went pretty much the same way most of these prisonbreak dime store novels go. What made this one different, is what one of them said about the breakout, like the psychology of it. He said, although the prick warden, the prick guards, and the whole institution had a million things to consider preventing an escape, the jailbirds only had *one* thing to consider—getting out. It was the advantage they had over everyone. I had told Logos about it, and maybe he saw it the way they did. Maybe it's what he was trying to tell me with his own breakout strategy of, "Play with nothing to lose." If so, it made a whole lot of sense, now.

§

Logos worked on the small generator, the long one, and now the fat one. His arms disappeared inside it.

I could barely see his head. "Need help? Do-you-need-help?"

He ignored me.

The fat generator took up half of the room. When he disappeared into its guts, I imagined him in blue surgical scrubs, under the hot surgical lights, doing a heart transplant. Well, the surgeon finally emerged from the generator, but in his old black mechanic's jumpsuit. He crawled out of that oven and bake at four hundred and fifty degrees for three hours, gasping. He was rundown and needed to rest. One more bit of magic, first; he pushed the red start button. The fat boy trembled, clickety-clanked, and pounded the ground like a train, *ump-ump-thump, ump-ump-thump.*

Progress, finally, and the blue camo called in. "Is good, good."

More squelching came over the radio. "Proceed, go." It sounded like Chicotte's voice.

Logos worked on the rest until we were done for the day. We loaded the toolbox into the bed of the jeep. Logos slipped out an unusual wrench and hid it in his rucksack. It looked like an ice tong but with two red tips.

"What's that for?" I said.

"Changing a timing belt. Land Rover by the trailer."

"Why?"

"In case we need an out." He threw me a harsh stare.

§

A bulky object sat inside his bag since boarding the plane but I couldn't tell what. When I asked him about it, he told me to mind my own business.

The blue camo driver shunted the jeep into gear. We drove back onto Main Street when the radio squelched on and he listened. He straightened his posture. "Yes, yes sir. I bring him now."

He slammed the gas pedal, and we played four-wheeler, rough and tumble, bumpety-bump over the terrain. It went on for as far as the eye could see. The KEM *was* a country within a country.

He stopped in front of Chicotte's office. "Go now!" the blue said to the brown. He pushed him by the nape toward the office, and it peeved him to wipe the man's sweat from his hand.

The brown camo went in.

We climbed out and headed for our trailer to rest when a shrill cry came from the office. We rushed there to see. When we asked the blue camo about it, he gave no reaction. He wiggled his fingers, shooing us away, and to vamoose to wherever we came from, and all. You see, his royal highness turned the seat of the jeep into his throne. This vane bastard reclined in it with his leg high on the dashboard, and his rifle pointed for us to go back to our shoebox for the night.

§

We walked to our trailer and kept our mouths shut. We did what we were told. We did our jobs. I never found out what happened to the brown camo, or the guard they tied up on the headframe, or Black Socrates. The guard they crucified on the old headframe always reminded me we would either end up as Workers or put way up there, too. It is the way of the gun here; the way of Chicotte.

Back in the trailer, time to rest. *Oh god, let me.* I fell asleep before my head even hit the pillow. Knocks, like rocks, pelted the door. What now?

15
THE VILLAGE

Someone always found another engine or dinosaur to exorcise out of death's grip. They were everywhere on the property, growing like weeds, only more difficult to remove. They needed Dr. Logos to remove them and leave the space better than he found it. He did it every time. He did it all. I only helped the best I could. When I couldn't throw some brawn in alongside his, I watched his back. When he finished the impossible, the men spoke to each other about him.

Through it all, I never forgot our predicament. I learned to work through it, to achieve something, maybe our freedom. During our first month, I kept my mouth shut, learned the discipline of work, to keep a schedule, to see the reality in front of me, not the one I imagined. I still did it at times, but the thing over us—the gloom—pushed it away.

§

Most times, I watched him work, unrelenting, uncompromising, a hurricane of energy and flesh. He saw the work in his mind, and after, it materialized in his hands. It made hundreds of men act, and those hundreds moved thousands, to give word the mine might run again, and the new shaft might pierce the ground, and make them rich. The final job hung overhead, too, along with the gloom.

The work resuscitated things, pumped new blood through corroded veins, and we inched closer to a history we talked about. I remember good days; I slurped black coffee and adrenaline for breakfast, high off it through lunch, coffee again, milestones met, and muscle collapse by dinner. Each day, one more item was scratched off the list. Each month, one more notch tied my belt tighter. They gave us enough food to keep going, but not enough to fatten a gut. Every Friday, Chicotte asked for Logos to turn in his broken stick, to be able to eat more, work less, rest on Sundays, have more assistants and less security, and sleep in a place where the snakes and rats didn't roam. Logos said no.

§

The months passed, and the work beat us down, but we never looked down, to say we were beaten, to say we were Workers. It would lighten the load on us if we chose it, and each man had to choose. Logos knew everything after would feel too heavy and impossible to live with, as subjects of the Masters. When you turned in your broken stick, and bowed, you turned in your self-esteem. You were no longer the same man. It would be too heavy to live with—heavier than taking on the additional work, and less food, and more punishment. Since we hadn't subjected ourselves, we weren't allowed to rest, couldn't look beyond the hard moment, where nothing looked bright, or promised anything, or took the fatigue away.

There was light. On some days, the sun set in a wide sky, and clouds lit up, electrocuted by wiry orange shards. It said another day was coming, or an escape plan, or something. After a few more months, we got used to it.

§

One day, work ended earlier than normal, and we rode back to Main Street in the jeep. The same blue camo prick drove, and Jando rode in the passenger seat. The bus which took the men back every day had left. We were taking Jando back to the village.

I asked him about Erik, whom I hadn't seen in weeks. He played coy in front of the guard. I asked him again. He shook his head for me to forget it.

I realized we hadn't been off the plateau since we got there, and I wondered if I would remember the outside. The driver told us to sit, it wouldn't take long, and don't try anything stupid and all. He still checked his nails every few minutes.

We drove until smoke corkscrewed over the tree line. Through the brush, a camp cut out of the density. An enormous barricade circled the village like a dam. A brown camo at the entrance clicked his head to the driver and we drove in.

A shantytown leaned over, ready to snap. Musk and woodsmoke intertwined overhead into an airy braid. Lines of thatched roofs and chicken wire for walls, made little box coops like a barracks, and people walked to and fro at an intersection like any big city block. This was the place where management mined the miners. It was rotting, and nothing had changed since they excavated the big hole. Nothing would change here.

Jando looked straight ahead. "There," he said, his voice flat, dead.

Another person spoke, compared to the one we met at the briefing. The jubilant boy, who liked to tell stories and baffle new friends, was gone. A quieter, introspective young man took up in him. "My place." He motioned to a box. The barricade rose behind and made an alleyway for all the coops. He jumped out. "Go back, now," he said to us. "Your job important. I go to rest." He was embarrassed.

A tall man stood in front of the hut. His eyes, vacant, and set deep beneath a wide forehead. Sand stuck to his skin. It was the man I had seen sleeping in fetal position with his tiny son, on the edge of one of the ponds, when we first arrived. It was Jando's father.

He waved at Jando. The little boy in fetal position from that day, held his hand.

The prick driver wagged his chin permission for us to go. "Hurry."

"Come," Jando said. "I show you, no?" He seemed reluctant.

We got out and ducked into the opening of the box. Pepsi advertisements made the wallpaper, hardened sand, the floor. Stars of light broke through the thatch roof, hardly adding light. A god-awful heat blew out.

"Come, come," his father said to us. He pulled the child in, the little arm, a tether.

"This where I sleep." Jando pointed to the flattened thatch. A faded poster of a soccer star kicking a goal hung overhead by string. The crowd cheered him. "We cook here." A campfire dug out of the silt next to it. "This my brother. Say hello." The boy shook hands with us.

His father, a string bean of a man, with softballs for shoulders, poured us some water. He wanted to share his food with us, but it was dark and hot and musty, and too small for this kind of gathering.

Logos didn't say a thing the entire time. He stepped out.

Jando's father nodded. His long bony fingers dragged across Jando's head, glad his son came home early. His brother pointed to his mouth, and his father brought him a plate of food.

Jando wouldn't keep eye contact with me. He bit his bottom lip. "Mr. Robert, you should go now." He shifted his feet. "The men wait, to celebrate for tomorrow."

Izbart had radioed the driver. All the workers had gathered, excited over the rapid progress Logos had made. Where the dinosaurs and peripheral equipment were supposed to take nine months to fix with all hands on deck, one man had done most of it in six. Tomorrow, the installation of Shaft #4, would begin. Below, was god only knowing. Everything went on the line.

§

Jando pressed his hand out for a reluctant shake. Our visit upset him.

"What's this?" I said.

"Nothing." He looked over my shoulder. "Must think about things. My father owe Chicotte the money."

Jando said they all came from the north, were promised jobs, a future, a contract. His father owed Chicotte twenty thousand dollars for it. Everything they got went to buy their food, firewood, and rent for the coop. and all sold by the KEM collective. I couldn't believe the last part—having to pay these pricks for a jailcell. What kind of hell was this? It cleared some things up—sure, but none of it any good. We were forced labor, Jando, and his father, bonded labor, or something.

He wouldn't look at me.

"Where's your mother?" I said.

He swallowed his saliva. "She, she die, Master." His gaze locked onto the dust at his feet.

"I'm no *Master*."

"Master" prompted him to look down. I told him not to do it, ever.

He looked at me for a long time. "Yes." He understood. "You are friend. My mother, she have trouble breathing one day after the work. The sun come down. She tired, very tired on this day. She did not wake."

"Did a doctor see her?"

He shook his head. He didn't want to talk about it anymore.

The driver curled his finger for us to come back, but I had to know about Erik.

Jando turned away from the guard. He told me Erik became scared after complaining to Mr. K. K. about not having enough helmets for the men. Erik disappeared days later. Jando looked into my eyes. "You can run, but they always find you." His voice quivered and the tears ran. He checked to see if the driver noticed.

I told him, he didn't.

Jando gathered himself. "Go, sir. I have things to do." His fist tapped his chin. He didn't want me to see him like this. He stared at the floor, again, the way Izbart often did. All the men looked to the ground when the old fear or "Master" summoned them.

The guard revved the engine to go.

"All right," I said. I shook his hand. "I'm sorry."

He looked away. His father cradled the little one.

I got into the back of the jeep. I couldn't speak.

§

Hundreds of men waited around the new headframe: T-shirted men, brown camos, a few white button-downs, and hardhats. They waved and we got out.

Izbart patted his heart. "To wish you the best of luck tomorrow."

Logos shook hands and whispered something to Izbart. They both looked at the men gathered at the headframe, and those men nodded back to Izbart. Simple faces looked back, expecting their world to change tomorrow. We didn't want to let them down. At this stage, they handed off their portion of the A-frame prep work and expected Logos to shoulder the rest.

It got late and we said our goodbyes. We made it to Chicotte's office before he locked up.

Inside, he played an odd game of scorpion ping-pong at his desk. A curly black scorpion waddled across expecting to hurdle the edge, but the wrestler's palm came up each time, prodding the critter to turn back.

They pinged and ponged, as his thick palm boomed up, and the thing hit headfirst against it.

"I'll need the phone tomorrow at three fifteen p.m.," Logos said.

"Work begins at six a.m.." He didn't look up.

The scorpion counterpunched, jabbed, and hooked, trying to sting Chicotte—but no way. Chicotte moved like a featherweight, coaxed like a politician, and peered like a warden.

Logos insisted on calling first, it'd be the last time he could call his bank.

What was the use? We couldn't collect the money but Logos pressed forward anyway.

Chicotte's thick palm came up again, corralling the critter toward a pine box. "*If* phone working." He shrugged, pouted, and couldn't give a crap. He boxed up the critter. You could hear the thing scratching inside. "Go sleep, now, my baby." He caressed the box. The big man took a moment to read the sludge and scabs over our bodies, as only new eyes can see old dirt. "Break your stick and bow." He waited for an answer.

Logos stared at Chicotte. An even harder streak revealed itself in Logos. He demanded the phones worked, and we were getting dicked around. It was a ballsy move.

"They work, *now*," Chicotte said, remembering. "We fix. Me forget." He dropped his head, signaling what he wanted us to do.

Logos wouldn't have any of it. "Calling to see if my three hundred grand's there."

"Very well." He bent a plastic smile.

"If it's in the account, I continue. Otherwise..."

My knees knocked like some old man.

Chicotte's nails tapped the desk, *clip-clop, clip-clop*. His eyes shifted about, anywhere to avoid ours. The map behind him caught his attention. When he looked back at us, his smile had shrunk, and the lips were flattened into drawn lines. He could see, without Logos on board, this ship was a sinker. He stood.

"Have no worries." He tapped his breast. "I will take care of this. We have deal. We respect deal. You do your work, and I see if I can help." His fingers sprinkled imaginary dust in the air to imply small potatoes.

What a relief.

"*Payment* is respect," Logos said.

What in the hell? It's the hard streak which kept re-surfacing like some submerged balloon. I hoped it might sink and never be seen again. In practical terms, there was no "deal." Chicotte could say anything, promise anything he damn well pleased. It didn't mean a thing; he played a game.

Logos was playing a game, too, and Chicotte liked—no, he loved the challenge. Few, if any, ever tried standing up to him, it seemed. He enjoyed the moment with a worthy adversary.

"Payment *is* respect. Yes." Chicotte erupted with laughter. "Ha. It is what I always tell the Mr. David. My friend, sometimes I like you." He reached over and slapped Logos hard on the shoulder. "We think same." Chicotte put out both his hands to shake like a pope. "Have no worries. I see what I can do."

"We want out of here."

"I will see. No promises."

It may turn out to be crap, but in the moment, it was light. My god, it felt good.

Logos walked out and I followed. We turned when we heard a ring—a jarring ring from the office.

"Listen to me." Chicotte shouted. "You have the cash, put it in."

We looked through the window, and plain as day, he talked on a phone. He hung it up and replaced it in the opening of the wall where the map once hung. He pushed the corner of the map back into its original place. Of course there were no phones (in sight), but phones-a-plenty behind maps, or desks, where the wrestlers and scorpions roam.

§

We made it to our trailer, barely. We were dragging serious ass, and my eyelids felt heavy.

"What can they do to us if we don't work?" I said.

"Don't know. It might get ugly."

I told him about Erik. He wasn't surprised. He reminded me of the run-in between Mr. K. K. and Erik in the briefing room. He reconciled these things as part of the KEM workcamp doctrine. He said it's something which happened out here, in this place, and we shouldn't read into it as Jando did, as this stuff went on between Masters and

Workers. We had our work, they had theirs, and leave it alone. We were still newbie foreigners—non-Workers. He summed it up: war and politics makes casualties, so don't be one.

I didn't get it. He pissed me off because what happened to Erik didn't piss him off as much. And what was all this pushback with Chicotte? His new demands threw our old exit strategy for a loop. Where did we stand?

He said he wouldn't begin the headframe work for Shaft #4 without the payment. He understood I pushed for the old plan, to finish the work, first. He said, to get respect, we would take a stand here.

I had theorized it had something to do with it but didn't expect it to be true.

He confirmed it. If they needed us, we stayed alive, and it somehow strengthened our standing in this place. Although they may kill the ones they love, they wouldn't kill the ones they needed. I hoped it was as simple as this.

"Increases our chances of staying alive?" I said. "By how much?"

"Oh, twenty, thirty percent."

"Vegas odds." It's better than nothing, all the way out here.

"They need to understand, a deal's a deal."

"These guys don't seem too understanding."

The old knees knocked, again, the stomach sank, and the sensation of free-fall. It felt the same way, even as far back as VMA, when these pricks locked me in the locker room overnight. It was freshman hazing, but if a kid was undersized like me, they doubled it. When the senior pricks grabbed me, and threw me in, the fear and gloom began. Ever since, I tried to control the temper which came with it. Each time the temper came so did something poisonous and witty out of my big mouth.

Quite a few people at VMA had accused me of being a sarcastic bastard. When they hazed me, and I couldn't fight back physically, I told them to go to hell for their family reunion, or some other banality. They had it coming to them and a whole lot more. Like I said, these guys at the academy were the biggest bag of pricks you've ever met.

In the halls and showers, they tried to provoke a scrap, so you had to hit them, this cabal of little shit rabble-rousers. It turned out to be a shakedown operation, as they blackmailed you for money. If you went to VMA, they knew your parents had bucks. So, cough up or explain to mommy and daddy why you're getting expelled for fighting.

Pricks. They're probably still snapping wet towels on people's asses. Ha, I'm here now and can't even remember any of their ugly mugs. I did remember to keep the sarcasm in check out here. Think before you speak, you know.

§

For now, I tried to work out our predicament the way Logos did. I could see the fear for what it was, an emotion, and it allowed me to at least see it was *something*. From there, you could sort of kick it in its butt. How? By solving the smaller problems which came with it, you broke down the big one. Instead of fearing the dark end—a bitch called death—you could focus on getting through the shock of the moment, the worry of the next hour, tomorrow, or next week. He described these as *tactics*, rather than *strategy*. This way, you could at least control the gloom in the short-term. His advice could work. At least it threw some cold water on the fear and all.

"They have to know they can't walk all over us," he said.

"The money part going to help us live longer?"

He said yes.

I could see where he went with it. It's what the money itself said: they needed us—or him, anyway. If they deposited it, we were valuable to them. It made sense in some way, even though actually collecting it wasn't in the cards. It seemed whipped, for now, not as scary, anyway.

"I have them right where I want them," he said.

"Where?"

"Over my knee." A palm made a paddle. "Spank, spank. A time comes when a man's premise is tested." He looked over at me, sure as hell the sun would rise, but hedging dawn with a bet, too. "Tomorrow's the day, brother."

Oh god, here we go.

16

CHECKMATE, SORT OF

The moment I lay down in my little bed for the night, Izbart called us back out. The compressor for the new headframe needed lubrication. It took several hours and turned a short day into a long day, which seemed like every other day.

When I lay down again, a phantom appeared. A black Logos stood at the door. Lube and tar covered him head-to-foot. I was full of it too. I hadn't even noticed. Oh man, if I only had a camera, holy crap. Well, we laughed about it, washed up, and I laid back down.

I woke up once or twice thinking about all the things which could go wrong in the morning. I worried about the money, not the dollars themselves, but what he said they stood for. If they respected you, they needed you. If they needed you, you stayed alive. Simple enough. Quite a trade: get some respect, stay alive. I wonder who came up with that one?

A flashlight shined on across the room. Logos kicked up his feet on a pillow and read *Building Mental Toughness*. In the dim, with its plain black cover, it could've been a Bible. It wasn't a Bible, though, and Father Manso would slap anyone's knuckles with a ruler if they said it. Maybe Logos's book taught someone how to think if they knew what to look for and how to use it. For those who did, perhaps it served as the "vaccine of the mind" to keep them alive out here.

"Going to take a walk," I said.

He never looked up.

§

Outside, the security was ever-present, and they upgraded the brown camos to blue camos by the door. I guess we were valuable commodities which needed safeguarding. One man's safeguarding is another man's prison, and the bars, gates, and locked doors simply divided the men, and the state of mind it put each man into, divided their thinking.

The nothingness beyond the mist still came down as a monolith, gray, quiet, but restless. The old fuzziness filled my head when I stared at it for too long. It was gloom and fear, too, only a different kind— fear of the unknown. Over the ridge, where the monolith came down, the moon hid behind a cloud bank. When it slid by, the mountain peak parted the clouds, brightening the sky.

"Out for a midnight stroll?"

It startled me.

Marc stood in the dark smoking one of his stogies. "Can't sleep?" His blink X-rayed me. "Leaner than when you first arrived."

"Garbage in, garbage out."

"Anemic. David Bowie, the Ziggy Stardust years. You know?"

I wanted to say something witty, but I did the old Ziplock on the lips.

"I hear you're doing a fine job," Marc said. "Extraordinary."

Without Logos around pressing his buttons, he seemed—what's the word...*charming*. He asked if I was up for a game of chess. I would think about it. Why the hesitation? None, I hadn't thought to play chess way the hell out here. Well, a game could be interesting, *way the hell out here*, right? It could work. Okay. I followed him into his trailer. He would look for the chessboard. Could I wait? Sure. He disappeared.

The shoebox looked like ours, only doublewide, and better furnished. A Persian rug, scarlet, covered the bare floor. Turner knockoffs and topographical maps hid the yellowed walls. The whole tin can was like a ship's cabin and lay soaked in an invisible sheet of moisture. My shirt stunk, now.

His desk sat across from me. A terrain of garbage cascaded down over one side. A petite white card, browned from age, nudged its head from the desk cover. I debated whether to read it. I sensed its personal nature. I couldn't resist.

To Anne:
Am I so rich with ambition,
I cannot stand with them?
Am I so poor with temptation,
I cannot resist a fem?
Do I bear so much ego
that I love when they lose?
The ambitious ones are the fakes,
and you I can no longer amuse.

You have been the fem I could never resist.
Love, M.G.

§

I was awash in guilt. I read it behind Marc's back. It was wrong—really wrong. Men of honor didn't act behind one another's back, reading their personal letters, or committing any unconfirmed act, no matter who they were. I didn't count myself amongst the *honorable* set, only a young man who now felt guilty. Perhaps he never sent the card, or he did, and she returned it. Maybe Anne meant something to him, but it turned out too late for him to be with her, so she moved on, or he moved on, losing her forever. I sensed a considerate, artistic side to him. No one could see it behind the pompous façade.

He reappeared, drying his hands. He opened a cupboard and extracted two plastic cups. "Oh, here it is." The chessboard came next. Marc placed it in front of me. He pointed to an obese jug sitting on the floor. "Wine or shine?"

"No—wait, you mean, moonshine?"

Clear fluid filled it halfway. Next to it, leaned a half-empty wine bottle sans label.

"I make the preferred blend for everyone."

"Isn't it a no-no here?"

"For whom? There are us and the others." One palm rose in the air, the other, lowered to his waist. "You see?" He poured from the jug.

I never touched my cup.

The chessboard resembled the one from the Villiers library; an old and ornate woody Staunton, designed for a king, or head of state to play on. I set the pieces. While in my palm, the black knight peered over at me in profile. The mane tousled in the imaginary wind, its mouth agape. I shifted the piece beneath the naked bulb. The eye opened and the pupil fully dilated. A cold black eye stared at me—a feral eye. My legs wobbled even while sitting.

My parents had given me a book as a toddler on the animal kingdom. A blackbird glowed in a halo on the cover, as if rising from the bowels of Hades. Although its eyes stopped me, their coldness held me prisoner. I was nauseated then and now. I saw it again in the knight. My heart beat faster, faster, blood coursed through my chest. The eye expanded, anxious, fearful of something, of me, of the unknown. Fear instigates fear—real or not. It spreads like a virus through the unprotected irrational mind. I faced the same thing when I first looked into the open pit mine, and into the mist beyond our trailer, and Chicotte's eye. Its nothingness evoked my fear. It's still in me, haunting me, guiding me, warning me—I didn't know why. I breathed and placed the knight back down.

He noticed something bothered me. "Everything on track for tomorrow?"

I caught my breath. "Looks like it."

He played white and moved first. He played a disciplined opening game and took central control of the board. I found it hard to keep up with him.

"How so?" he said. He knew he got me locked up.

I tried to forget the eye. "Logos completed pretty much everything."

Some knew this, some didn't.

He looked up at me from his pieces. "The drill bit to twister plate, can he connect it?" He thought he discovered treasure and could pump me for information.

Well, I let him, but I gave him pennies, not dollars. I didn't know about the connecting plate with certainty, I said. The drill bits were custom, the attaching plates as well, only Logos knew.

Marc kept it up and turned a friendly game into a friendly interrogation. He wanted to know what was deepest in Logos's mind, deepest in his heart.

I told him, again, I wasn't sure.

"Quite talkative last time with his, 'Without me you're nowhere stuff. I'm this, I'm that'—with his bollocks about a syllogism."

He caught Logos on a bad day, I said. If the stars aligned, and he felt generous, Logos could talk freely, even let someone inside. It wasn't often.

"He's derisive, Robert. Don't think everyone likes him." He paused, looked down at my pieces.

I left my knight hanging as sacrificial bait. I was worried I'd made a mistake, but I thought about it. It was straight math but a gambit. If he took it, it'd give me a better position later. I waited...waited...he salivated over it—he took it. It cost me a valuable piece but left his king file vulnerable. I unleashed hell on it.

His face turned sour. "Nasty ambush."

I gloated inside.

He looked out the window. Except for our trailer light, a black fog had fallen over the pathway. The blue camo guard stood by the door.

"Robert, not feeling well." He tossed his arms up.

"You resign?"

He stood. "Of course not! I'm ill." The back of his hand checked his forehead for a temperature, flailing like a fish. He crinkled up his lips at the result. "Certifiably ill."

Yes, by god, he had come down with a fever in only ten minutes. Odd, certainly, and some medical journal would surely need referencing. He would do it at once.

I got up. "All right-y. Got to go." I wanted out.

"Sure about tomorrow? It'll be done?"

I nodded.

"I'm feeling better already." The flailing fish gestured to the heavens.

§

I made my way down the cinderblock steps. I wanted to get out. *Move*.

"You know," he said, "I'm the one who found the deposit—the kimberlite."

"You're great." I was willing to say anything to get me passage off this sinker.

Marc came alive again. The compliment, although patronizing, sufficed to cure his ailment, and the medical journal wouldn't need referencing after all. He hadn't heard a compliment in years, he said, even this kind. He thanked me, all sugary and polite as royalty.

To his point about the discovery, I pushed back. An independent geological survey had been done first.

He said he found the samples *first* and informed David they should have the study done only after. "Don't you believe me?"

I shrugged.

"Good night." He said he'd be there tomorrow. He remembered something. "Tell Logos, he'll need me. I know the exact spot to drill. Good night. I do feel so much better."

Marc stood over the chessboard, pinkie finger to mouth. He unleashed a backhand—the board flew—a violent crash. Pieces hung in the air and bounced off his forehead like pinball. He stood, hands on hips, looking at the empty table.

If you're a competitive bastard, and you lose to someone in a chess match, it can feel like they own your soul. Tomorrow was life or death, we knew it, but I fell asleep straightaway, grin on my face.

17
THE BEST KEPT SECRET IN THE DRC

I was dreaming with the chess gods until I wasn't.
    Two camos shook the bejesus out of us and dragged us out of bed, to the path in front of our trailer. I didn't recognize any of them, but they were armed and sent there to take us somewhere. One of the KEM jeeps parked in the middle of the path, lit up silver in the moonlight. We heard another engine knocking, and Chicotte pulled up behind it. He came alone.

    He got out, casual and cheery, like taking a walk in La Fontaine or Central Park on a sunny day, no care in the world. He had on his beret, slipped to one side. The person he wanted for this late night meeting was Logos. He put his paw-hand on Logos's shoulder. "I want to show you something, my friend." He squeezed his shoulder and made a mechanical smile. He told me I would be going along.

    Logos and I looked at each other.

§

    Chicotte rode off first, and we followed in the jeep behind him, with the two new camos in front. We drove bumpety-bump over the same terrain and trail we had been on when Logos worked on the generators, leading us to the other side of the property. No one would say exactly where on the other side we were going or why. We were to shut-up, sit back, and wait.

    Chicotte cut through the trail and ducked a few branches which wanted to take his head off. We lost sight of him, with only his taillights poking through the thick cover. He didn't need to slow down, though, as our driver knew where to go. I looked over at Logos, and he took a deep breath. Was I worried? Yes, I was worried.

§

Things look different in the night. There aren't the steep cliffs to see down into the valley, and risks can't be seen coming around the corners, and speed can't be judged, so as to not be thrown from the back of the jeep. It's scarier at night because you lose a dimension in space. The sky and ground are nearly the same color, especially at high speeds. As we cut through the bush, we could hear the arrogant laughs of the hyenas, and the growls of lions, and the relentless bush crickets playing their violins. But what's truly scary is what can't be seen. It is waiting and can wait all night and would reveal itself only when the jeep actually stopped.

I grew restless listening to this cacophony and waiting for the jeep to stop. I raged inside. Someone needed to take action. I wanted to smash the driver's face, take the wheel, and crash at whatever the cost. Logos noticed the old Mr. Hyde building inside me and told me to relax. We would work this out. He worked it out before, and he would work it out again. *They needed him more alive than dead, remember?*

How much could you trust another man? I had to trust him all the way, I guess, there were only two of us. He got us this far, and we were still in one piece. I took a deep breath, too, and it took the edge off. I wondered if the animals were trying to warn us in their own languages about where Chicotte was taking us. Maybe they knew, but we would find out soon enough.

§

The knoll in the road came up where the brown camo had lost his radio on our first day out. I knew we were on it. I could see the generator room from the top of the mound, lit by long yellow fluorescents beneath its eave. Across the generator room, the radio-room prison was lit by a single bulb swaying over the door. We stopped there, and they told us to get out. Chicotte had already parked on the side of the dirt path. The camos motioned for us to approach the door. The blue camo driver stunk of cigar smoke, and his breath stunk even worse.

Chicotte got out of the jeep. He pointed at the door. "Here we are, my friends." Two more camo guards walked behind him.

"What in the hell's this?" Logos said.

There were bars over the door. Chicotte took out a ring full of odd-shaped keys like something an old warden might carry around. He told the guards to stand behind us and cover the escape flanks. He unlocked the door and motioned for us to enter.

"This is where we keep the smart people, like you."

"I thought we had a deal."

"Punishment makes respect." He laughed. "It is the deal." The two camos followed his lead and smirked. "You had good deal. Air to breathe, bed to sleep. Now, you will see what a bad deal is. Go." He wasn't laughing anymore.

The two camos came up and pushed us through. We fell over the doorstep and tried to get up. The deadbolts slammed shut.

We heard the jeeps drive-off.

"Fucking prick!" I said. "Now what?"

"Now, nothing. We wait."

Logos looked around the room. The moonlight slanted in through the barred window, leaving three dark shafts from the bars over the floor. There were no beds, or tables, or cable TV, only an inch of dust which kept us coughing and sneezing until the morning came around. The two guards stayed outside taking turns looking in on us through the window. We weren't going anywhere any time soon.

I would try and make the best of it, though. I was wiped out. If you can't run, and can't work, at least rest. I laid on my back with my fingers intertwined behind my head as a pillow for the entire night.

§

When I woke the next morning, I foot-long caterpillar was making its way over my foot. Holy crap. I jumped up and shook. Logos laughed like crazy.

Even though I snoozed off and on the entire night, I was more tired than before. Logos barely slept, he said. He got up before me and stood looking out the window. He was beaten down, I could tell, although he wouldn't admit it.

From the window, other barred windows were visible. We yelled for anyone who might be there. Logos said to wait, yelled again, but no one responded. I remembered a thick antenna poked out of the center of the building from when we first came. It was tethered to four ground stakes, two of which we could see at the edges of the cleared area around the building.

No jailbirds had been locked-up in this place for years, maybe even decades. How long would we be here? No one could answer that call either. One thing was certain, there wasn't a deal in place to get us free. It was simply talk, like everything else was talk, and talk meant diddly-squat. Chicotte was making the lesson about respect into a field trip. This was about us respecting *them*.

I asked Logos if we were done for.

He had regained his composure and paced the ten by ten cell. He told me to look around. We weren't injured and the connection for Shaft #4 hadn't been done yet, he said. They had shot themselves in the foot by putting us out here. Why, Dr. Logos? Well, nurse assistant, Bonhomme, I'll tell you why: there was no one else to connect the drill bits to the plate to rain down money on this place and make it fertile again. The longer they kept us here, the longer their temple would stand idle, and the king would harangue Chicotte for putting them behind schedule. See? Oh, yes, I see. He was right, as usual.

§

The next morning, a camo dropped us off two bowls of food, which he pushed beneath the door. It was a reddish soup of sorts, vegetables, grasshoppers, dried up caterpillars, and rocky cassava, all mixed together and sprinkled with paprika like goulash. Man, we were so hungry, we ate it all, legs, tails, and curved bodies to boot. After a while, a new energy took up in us. It turns out, most families in Kinshasa eat about a half a pound of insects per week as part of their nutrition. It's hearty, cheap, and easy to come by.

The camo who brought the soup stood around and waited for us to finish, so as to get the bowls and spoons back.

Logos told me to notice something. The soup was steaming hot.

"Yeah, so what?"

"It means someone *cares* if it's hot or not. It's not an accident.

Bacteria has a danger zone, doubling every twenty minutes if not killed by heat. Someone's watching over us. They need us, still, or we'd be eating raw grasshoppers, or caterpillars, or cold mystery meat, or nothing at all. Got me?"

Man, when they need you, they need you, and you get the good hot stuff, and stay alive.

The camo asked Logos if he was the great man everyone said he was, especially Izbart.

"I don't know," Logos said. "I'm here like you, trying to get through it."

The guard looked around to make sure they were alone. "There is a man who believes you are, Izbart. He is willing to place himself at risk for you."

"I see."

"Many guards believe in him. He is a Worker above all types of men."

"Above? How?"

"He is a good man. The last good man here. The one we trust."

Logos thanked him for the soup. "If he is a good man, listen to him."

The guard said he would. He got back into his jeep and drove. He waved goodbye, leaving a screen of dust behind.

§

Logos patted his belly. He sat, back to the wall, elbows over his knees, to think this situation through. He did the same thing on the plane from New Hope to the Café KEM, the best kept culinary secret in the DRC. He let go the longest belch I ever heard, and I laughed to myself. I knew we would be fine for now, or for at least the next few days.

We sat around and shot the shit for the whole day. In all truthfulness, it was the most rest we had in the six months we'd been here. In a way, I appreciated the cell for the rest it allowed us.

The same camo guard brought us dinner. He said Izbart said hello, and not to worry, we were good men too. We would be back sooner than his lost oxen Juni, whom his neighbor found in their backyard one day. Enjoy the time at the resort, and the café, and such. We told the guard to thank him.

The bush crickets revved up their symphony and we slept until morning.

§

The two camos who guarded us, showed up at noon. They held the warden's ring of keys, let us out, and took us back to our trailer. We were to stay inside until tomorrow, when the final work would begin, inaugurating the temple and everything we hoped for. This time, they marched up and down the path in front of our trailer, occasionally looking in on us.

18
INAUGURATING THE TEMPLE

Dawn. A chill came over me when I realized Logos was gone. I imagined him crashing through the front gate in the Land Rover like a madman and leaving me behind. I couldn't believe he would leave me hanging—no way, especially after all we'd gone through. He'd promised me too much. Hell, we were blood brothers after the pact we made to see this thing through. There was no way he would leave me.

The headframe connection would begin later, and the whole place depended on him, too. The thought of us finally working way up there on the platform made me pause, and I detected an anxious ticking in me. No one knew if the connection could work, and what it might cost the good citizens of the Ville, if it didn't. The ticking told me, the connection's a gamble; place our chips on a single number—hit, and walk away free men, miss—castigated, or worse, gone bye-bye. It fell on Logos to make it happen, and we all placed too much in his hands at times. It was downright sadistic, but he handled it like few men could, and better than a dozen Masters, or Workers ever could. No one knew the future, though, not even him.

I went to look for him outside.

The daybreak softened everything, and old objects appeared new and different. My boy, Logos, stood in front of the old Land Rover. Whew. The blue camo guard kept asking him what he was up to. Logos ignored him, lost in the depths of the engine.

The truck sat on four inflated tires now. He placed the ice tong wrench inside the engine for a time and removed a square board from his rucksack. He knelt with the board as if consoling an icon. He held the gear-faced clock which once hung in his office. He pried the smaller gear off the clock and placed it into the engine. The larger gear, which made the clock's face, remained. He made adjustments to the engine—and boom. It started. The clock went back into the rucksack. He buried the keys to the truck while the blue camo puffed away on a dart. Yes siree, I witnessed part of his masterplan in action. He hedged the headframe risk with an escape vehicle in case things didn't go so well later.

Izbart came by, and they discussed something. Actually, Logos talked, and Izbart listened. Logos handed him a slip of paper. They shook hands, and Izbart tapped his heart to say thanks.

§

By three p.m., we stood in Chicotte's office. The map was taped back, and all looked nice and tidy. An old rotary dialer phone sat on the foldout desk, everything else cleared away. Guess what? The phone worked. We acted all surprised—a miracle. When Logos confirmed the money in his account there was no acting—it shocked us. Although the radio room-prison put the scare in us, Chicotte knew the money would keep Logos chipper and working in everyone's best interest. It probably amounted to tipping the waiter if this thing rained down money the way everyone expected. We speculated about his motivation, of course, and no one knew for certain. Oddly, when I called my bank, static came over the line.

A blank look came over Chicotte's face.

"You need to pay both of us," Logos said.

"We check tomorrow again. So..." Chicotte pointed at the door. "Let us begin."

Logos got paid, and man, it meant something; we would live another day.

On our way to the headframe, I asked Logos about my deposit. He promised me one half of his wire if I didn't get mine, as serious, and plain-faced as anyone I ever met. I got all choked up. It was a good thing, since it kept me from asking about the Land Rover.

Chicotte sashayed past, reeking of sweat. The big man could get a move on when he needed to. He shook hands with the Workers, or patted their backs with heavy palms, knocking them off balance. I figured it was an act, a sort of political currency he doled out to everyone to make himself like one of the gang. One time—and it blew me away—I saw him and Mr. K. K. freeing a baby gazelle caught up in the barbed wire. It must have lost its way at night. The whole crew watched. Anyway, Chicotte released it. Mr. K. K. checked its vitals, while the big man pet it, and they both tapped its rump to go. I was speechless. Here were these guys, brutal to all mankind, but gentle to animals. They said the top of the KEM hierarchy loved animals but hated people.

§

At the foot of the headframe, fewer men gathered around compared to yesterday. With everything it took to get us here, and the anticipation in the village, I expected a ticker-tape parade, or at least the Canadian Derby. I was wrong again. Only a dozen workers lingered around the yard. They paced near the shiny temple, raising and lowering their gaze at the party of button-downs standing ahead of us. Everyone smoked.

One man exhaled, and the puff erased his face. Another looked straight at Logos. "We are with you," he said. The other Workers nodded. Chicotte gave them the old stink face.

Logos nodded back to them.

Marc and Izbart stood at the foot of the zigzagging stairs which led to the top. Izbart nodded to us.

Chicotte came by. "*Gentlemens. My best, best* wishes." He gave a thumbs-up, stretching the sleeve of his blue camo.

"Best of luck to us all," Marc said.

Logos went up the stairs and I followed.

One leg lifted and fell, until we stood on a catwalk beneath the top floor. The whole zigzagging stairway shook as if attached by a thread. We stood at nearly the highest point over the plateau. The full land came into view: the giant hole, the barbed fence surrounding us, the acacia tree canopy, water running below, shiny, splintery, and silver.

Mr. K. K. already stood at the top, as well. He was singing his favorite song, again. He kept on eye on us, but there didn't seem to be a good reason why. What was a Master guarding up there? There wasn't anywhere we could run to or anything to steal. It made me think.

Izbart came up and gave instructions to the six of us who stood around the giant housing for the hoist. It would bring up the plate connection for the drill bit. The black cable moved up one side of the pulley and down the other.

I held the installation sequence Logos outlined to me earlier: drill bits to plate, plate to drill rod, check fittings, pressure test, calibration.

Mr. K. K. glimpsed at me. "Stand here." He wanted me closer to the hoist, near the edge of the platform.

"He's good where he is," Logos said, as he slipped on his gloves. "Stay there."

I studied his hand-drawn engineering plans. The detail couldn't be believed, the steadiness of the hand, out of this world. The drawn parts appeared as if from a printer.

The hoist gear whined, spun faster. Voices ricocheted. Logos peeked down to see why. Mr. K. K. looked at me; his eyes pulsed. I had a bad feeling, like when we first got in the old Lincoln for the airstrip. He rushed at me—everything went black.

§

Feet scuffled by, and there were calls for help. The light came. My head lay on the cold steel sub-platform. The same people and place surrounded me but further into the future. The present had leapfrogged forward like a jump cut in a film. The next thing I remember, people stood over me looking into my eyes. My forearm split from some alien pain. I tried to grab it—but it wasn't there. About a million things went through my old noggin, and most of it wasn't any good. Someone lifted it and placed a soft rolled object beneath, but I couldn't move it to see my arm.

Jando and Izbart looked after me, and Izbart talked on his radio.

I tried to get up but couldn't.

Sounds bent and slurred from mouths. "Staaay...doooown...Mr. *Robert*," Jando said. His hardhat fell over his eyes.

Time slowed.

Logos argued with Mr. K. K. "The...most...despicable...thing I've ever...seeeen," Logos said.

"Where's...my...arm? Did I lose it?" I hyperventilated.

Old Father Time still limped along in slo-mo, bending voices into pretzels.

Izbart paced back and forth at my feet. "*Calm...doooown...*" he said.

Someone must've pressed the fast-forward because it all sped back up. It hit me. My arm—what in the hell happened to it? "Oh, my god, oh my god." My ribcage caved in.

Izbart looked at where my arm was supposed to be. "We get you help, now."

"Tell me!" I cried.

Stupid kid. Twenty-one years old, and all the rash decisions I ever made in my life crashed down on me. I was wrong from the start about it; wrong for going along on this thing; wrong for believing something could come of it; wrong for acting like a high roller who thought he was going to suck the world down like an oyster. I always dreamt of becoming one of those men you read about who accomplished something so great in their lives it could never be topped. It was all bullshit. I tried to impress myself the whole time or any old fool who'd listen. Fake it until you make it and crap. But there's no faking life; you don't suck it down, it sucks *you* down. In the end, the only person you fool is yourself. I made mistakes. We all make mistakes. Our own fuckups are the hardest to swallow.

§

Jando bit his lip, patted my cheek. "You be okay, my friend." He tried to comfort me, but it only added to the ticking in my chest.

"Is there b...blood?" I couldn't lift my head to see. *Goddammit.*

"Some, some blood."

I knew he lied.

"Get someone now!" he said to someone.

Izbart stood over me. He told me to stay down, called me a good boy and stuff. I was glad to have someone to look after me, and gladder it was him. His presence calmed me.

But who was I kidding? I knew the score; my life was over. It was ending here, on the cold steel, in the middle of this thing, away from family, friends, and home, and forced to watch as its prisoner. No one would ever know the truth about what happened to us, because there was no one to tell them. It's like we were vaporized. *Robbie-boy, you had a good run. You need to accept this.* The red stuff flowed out. I had to ask, "Am I...dying?"

"We compressing the blood," Izbart said. His cheeks puffed with air.

Yeah man, it was over.

Logos got in Mr. K. K.'s face. "I saw you," he said.

The old man threw his arms up. "What you see, huh? What?" The taped-up Kalashnikov flapped over his shoulder. He wouldn't give an inch.

"You hit him in the head and cut him."

Mr. K. K. spat on the ground as he descended the stairs. "You see nothing."

Two hardhats pointed at him. "Master, why?" yelled one.

Mr. K. K. made a gun out of his hand and pointed it at the man. He cast his black eyes over Logos like a net. They could freeze a prey, the gaze, cold, heavy, and entangling. If someone realized it, it was too late.

"Turn around," Logos said, following him down. "Don't look at me!"

The hardhats looked at each other, shocked.

"I said, don't look at me." Logos spoke in a controlled voice, and although softer, it grew powerful. "You will listen to me, old man." Logos had the biggest balls of anyone in this country.

The old man turned away, finally, and grinned as he moved.

The Workers watched and whispered to each other about Logos. I doubt any of them had ever heard someone stand up to a Master the way he did.

"I don't feel too good," I said.

My shutters closed.

19
Helmets, Cars, and Girlfriends

I woke up at some field hospital, and a young Congolese nurse told me I wasn't dead. I laid on my back but couldn't see the rest of me. My head weighed more than the universe.

They brought me to MAI to recuperate. My body felt disconnected, like when a magician cuts his assistant into two during a magic trick and separates them on stage. I was in one piece, though. You see, my head was strapped in some kind of brace-helmet. It made a silver-framed window for me to see out of, as if I were wearing a helmet. I watched the breeze make waves on the underside of a gigantic tent. The taut canvas fluttered and flapped, light blue with the logo of a cross going down its center.

There were plenty of others around, probably in cots too, but I couldn't see them. I heard their heavy coughs, whispers, smelled rubbing alcohol, felt the clammy heat over me. My nurse's cherub cheeks filled my frame. She said I needed to stay put for a while, and the doctor would come.

Later, another woman came to check on me. She wasn't a nurse or anything and wore a T-shirt with the same light blue cross printed on all sides.

"Do you know where you are?" she said.

"Hospital." I heard her soft voice before, but where?

"What happened to you?"

"Accident." It's all I could muster.

"Quite serious." Her eyebrows flattened. They were fair and the same color as her forehead. "Remember me?"

I shook my head "no," but it didn't move. The head brace-helmet kept it firm.

A natural glow radiated from her skin and straight blond hair. She had a pretty face, one of those which become ugly if there's too much make-up on it. She knew better and kept it clean, which showed it natural, and it stayed beautiful. I liked looking at her, and she reminded me of my ex-girlfriend Lauren.

I dated Lauren before I left New York and had to break it off with her, even though I didn't like it. I couldn't fake a relationship while I was about a million miles away. Anyway, I missed her now. I missed the things she did and said and the things we did together.

She was a strange girl, and I guess I dated enough of them by now, to say, I like them strange. It's just me. She never drank coffee, or went to the gym, and hated wearing pumps—I mean hated them like a woman's plague. She was more of a flower power empathic type with a model's face. The face was so good, the whole time I dated her, I kept a pic of her in my car. Come to think of it, she gave me one to put there. Maybe she saw it as marking her territory or something. Anyway, she took one of those cliché photobooth pics—the ones where everyone mugs it up too much—and cut it into the size of a quarter and asked me to keep it near the radio. I stuck it onto the radio volume, so when I turned the tunes up, her face spun around. I met her around the time I first met Logos. Was it her? The old shutters closed.

§

I must've been under heavy meds, because I drifted back to months before we ever left for here. At the time, I almost got evicted from my dumpy studio apartment in Astoria. It was after my family's financial woes.

Logos had already paid me in cash for consulting on his employment contract. I needed it, too. It got me out of hock with my landlord and car's storage facility. I needed to pick up the car and deposit the money he paid me in my bank. I wasn't the type who left cash lying around, especially wads of it.

I left his shop excited to finally drive the last remnant of a privileged youth, my 1980 Porsche 928. The spaceship body still looked great even though it was fourteen years old. Only the motor was done for and needed a genius to resuscitate it. Even during my darkest days,

I never thought about selling her—wouldn't, couldn't—even for all the relief money in the world. So, I decided to make a day of it; drive my old car, deposit the cash, and see the city.

Logos waited at the front of the shop. He motioned to the car behind door number one and all. The car sat brooding in idle. It was a symphony for the right ear, and I knew he'd fixed her right.

"I'll be taking her," I said.

The streets sat empty for the long President's Day weekend. They waited for me and my gal: lead foot and Porsche. *Got to go, got to go.*

Logos extended his hand. We shook, a sturdy but not forced handshake. I hate those hand-breakers people do when shaking to impress. He wasn't trying to prove anything.

"You deserve it," he said.

"I do."

He raised his arm, bestowing a benediction, "See you."

From the window, I could already see Lauren's pic flaked off the radio knob. What a face. It really did seem cut out from the cover of one of those fashion magazines you see cluttering a newsstand. I wondered why her face wasn't actually doing the cluttering. She'd tried modeling, but her school took up all her free time. Her real name was Astrid, but everyone called her Lauren. When her family first moved to New York from Germany, her teachers had trouble pronouncing her real name correctly.

I opened the door. My car seat had the congruency of an old girlfriend, too, and I hoped she felt the same way. I kept the radio off. I turned the ignition—bang. I opened her up on thirty-first street before any red lights blinked on. The wheels clasped the pavement. I didn't need or want anything on this drive. I was complete as a man, on this road, this pavement, this drive. We passed sixty. The engine and exhaust purred something magical when my foot pressed the gas. "I am with you!" she said, "I am yours." Off we went.

Driving is man's escape at times. I needed to drive and for a long time. I wanted to spend the rest of the day reuniting with her, to see the city together. I would drive and she would run.

§

I made it over the RFK bridge into Manhattan and looked for a clean empty garage to park my girl. I preferred a newer one, where no jalopies were allowed. I found a five-star spot, pulled in nice and slow, and tucked her away at the end of the row. Rest up. Be back soon. It sounds moronic, but I gave the doorframe a kiss goodbye, too.

On Fifth Avenue and forty-sixth street, past Dr. Greenberg's gold chiropractor shingle, and the Chinese takeout, hung the sign for the jazz club, Blackbird's. I'd never been there, as everyone always told me the door cover was twenty bucks, and I could use those funds better elsewhere. Anyway, the sign always got me as I passed. When the neon flickered off, a dark bird slept like a canary. When it came on, a spark electrocuted the hawk's ruby eye to alert. The eye glowed big-small, big—small. A man sweeping the doorway below it noticed me, and we exchanged an uneasy glance.

The air cooled. The grim gray rolled in, and store lights popped on like popcorns filling the street. I may as well've been in Miami. My own sun shone and followed me wherever I went as I made my way up Fifth holding five thousand in my breast pocket. My bank's main branch came up, lit up like Christmas.

I met Lauren there for the first time. She worked as a teller. I'd been there once before and loved the feeling inside. The grand foyer made you feel richer. I figured those architects, with their tortoise-shelled spectacles, planned it to get people's money. The scale of it—everything was bigger, nicer, richer. Manhattan always kicked ass. A provincial mindset came over the smaller borough branches, where I was overlooked, even invisible. Better-looking girls worked in the city, too.

One of them, a gorgeous siren, called me to the window. "Can I help you?" She stared at my mouth.

She was tall, with dirty blond hair parted straight down the middle. Something about those long equivalent strands fired me up. I made my deposit and asked her out for lunch. She said no. The following week, I asked again, and she said yes.

I looked forward to the date all week, and a little friend of mine, Mr. Narcissism, agreed, people would see me *with* her. We hit it off from there, and I had the best two months of my life. She distanced herself when I told her about me going overseas to work with Logos. What could I do? I needed the money. I had to make a major decision. I didn't regret leaving on the trip at the time. It was the most important decision

I ever made. I only regretted where I ended up and I missed her. It's the way it is, though. So, for now, enjoy those nights and days in strange loving arms while you can, as they don't always last.

§

"Robert, Robert Bonhomme!" The blond lady in the T-shirt shook my shoulders. The underside of the tent flapped in the breeze behind her ear. "Wake up, please."

The young Congolese nurse stood next to her holding a block of sheets. They waited for me to speak.

My mouth moved but nothing came out.

20
A TEMPORARY STATE OF AFFAIRS

The blond woman waved her hand across my face. "Wake up!" She shook me. "Know where you are?"

I snapped awake. "Hospital."

"You see? The man knows," the Congolese nurse behind her said.

"Fine," the blond woman replied.

I wasn't on a date. I wasn't in New York and it wasn't my Lauren. My head still couldn't move from the brace, and the silver-frame limited my view.

"I call doctor." The Congolese nurse moved out of my frame.

Everyone who looked at me kept saying I shouldn't worry. A veritable pep squad came by, "You're fine," "He's okay," and my favorite, "It's a temporary state of affairs," as one doctor put it. It made me worry even more. I should trust the consensus, but I never have, never will. I guess it's how I ended up a prisoner in the DRC, lying flat on my back, in a field hospital, wearing a head brace, with a lovely nurse looking into my eyes.

The day passed. The tent flapped and waved. Below it, an intricate network of poles ran like plumbing, and I wondered how many poles made all the connections, and how much they all weighed and cost. A breeze grazed the canvas and left ripples like the wide ocean.

Voices and equipment rattled by, birds chirped, a cacophony of coughs, too. On top of everything else, they must've given me too many muscle relaxers. I couldn't give a crap about anything, and I floated in and out of catnaps. I didn't feel right.

§

A long Errol Flynn nose pushed the tent out from view and spoke. "Suffered a grade two concussion, moderate, when you fell." It said these words thousands of times to thousands of others. "Keeping your head stable, few days only. Nothing to worry about. A temporary state of affairs."

Oh god. I panicked about my arm. "I can't see it."

I imagined myself twenty years in the future without it. I walked up and down Fifth Avenue, again, but hungry, in ragged clothes, one empty sleeve flapping in the breeze. I begged people for change like an old gutter pup. *Calm down,* I thought. *Get the facts, first, man.* Ask and you shall receive.

"It's fine," the nose said. "Wait." He pushed a thick gauzed limb to my face.

I had my ole boy. I missed you. I had my arm. I thanked all the powers: God up in the clouds, my parents, my buddies, my doctors, my instructors at Villiers (they weren't so bad now), those pricks in the showers and hallways, the NYU crew, Logos, Izbart, Jando, this cot, the tent, the Congolese nurse—especially her. I breathed fuller; the air smelled fresher. I saw the richness of colors.

"Bad laceration, forty-four stitches. You're the new record."

The nose drew back. The man attached to it had olive skin and thick salt and pepper hair. He spoke with a Spanish accent. Yes, the doctor we met in Kindu...um...um, Dr. Ramirez, yes. He and the blond woman, Eden, wore matching T-shirts in the market, yes, yes. At the time, they struck me as movie stars, do-gooder versions of Bogie and Bacall, who wandered off the set between takes, and into the wasteland to see us little people.

"We met across from the market," I said.

"Correct."

When we first met, I thought he was as old as can be. I'll never be so old. But, after delivering my arm back in one piece, he was a young stud, always and forever.

Eden stood sideways at the foot of my cot. She tilted her chin down, squeezed her eyes, like a batter waiting for the pitch. She didn't actually stand like a baseball player; it was only the expression on her face.

"So, Doctor," she said, "is this young man going to make it back to Montreal?"

She and Ramirez shared some inside joke about my head brace-helmet and baseball, and would I ever be able to screw the young ladies again and all. (By the way, they said I still could). Anyway, I could see why Logos liked her. Her beauty attracted you, and the playful girl inside her kept you glued, and you loved her for it.

Ramirez said I had more than a fighting chance. He told me two days had past. It may as well've been two weeks or two months. Time collapsed, or expanded, or didn't mean a damned thing.

"You have a visitor," Dr. Ramirez said. He must've stood, as I could only hear him.

The doctor pat my leg goodbye. "Figure you'll need a few more days here."

"Thanks again!" I yelled, too loudly.

Logos's face popped in the screen. A friend came to see me, and it felt as close as family. The gloom lifted some.

He kept a straight face. "Vacation, huh?"

I told him I barely missed the big sleep.

He crept a smile. "Pack your bag. Private jet's on the tarmac."

"I doubt it."

"So do I."

He looked fine, but multiple things ran in his mind day and night, taking care of a kid wasn't one of them. Anyone could see it. At times, his attention would drift to those handful of things which plagued and inspired a man like him: the mine, his work, all the crap he did in South America before we ever met and never talked about, our captivity, Eden, and perhaps some exotic place he could run away to in his mind, and find refuge in.

I was a weight on him. I could see it, yet I tried to bring him back to now. "You attach the drill bit?"

He couldn't, he said. Something blocked one of the attaching holes in the plate. He looked around for his refuge, again. "Let's talk about it later."

We knew the drill bit connection would be tricky. For god's sake, it came with no instructions, no training, no engineering plans. He was improvising, off the cuff, a magician on the road who lost all his props. He assured me, nothing's broken, nothing to worry about there. Chicotte was steamed we fell behind. Logos tapped his own temple. He knew I knew there was a screw loose in the wrestler, but no one else would talk about it.

"They closed the gates," he said. "No one's allowed off the property until I connect it."

The village had been cut off, too. No vehicles, food, or water could go in or out. Chicotte would sacrifice them for Logos's mistake. It didn't seem *fair*, but the word lost its currency the day we boarded the plane.

"Wait, you said something blocked the bit going into the plate?"

Footsteps approached and he waited to answer. Logos told me what I already presumed. He planned out the connection well, meticulous to a fault, yet something else prevented a proper fit. The tooling of the parts could've been off, or they were tampered with. Maybe someone didn't want Shaft #4 to find the sweet spot in the earth and rain down the sort of wealth others dreamed of. They liked things the way they were. Could it be...

"Sabotage," he whispered. "Maybe."

"It's not your fault."

"Doesn't matter. As far as Chicotte's concerned, burden's on me."

I urged him to try again, knowing he could do it. He didn't need a cheerleader, far from it. He wasn't the type. I needed him to hear me say I wouldn't give up on him the way he never gave up on me. I got it off my conscious like confession and felt lighter.

I thought about the sabotage, and something David had said to Logos in the office the day we met him. "There are those who seek the truth, while some want to believe." Nietzsche first said it, and although I wasn't a fan of his, the observation couldn't be denied. My thinking changed. Facts equaled truth, and reality displaced the darkness of blind belief. Reason was the flashlight guiding you through. It guided you through the murk of fear. Logos had a reason—a set of facts—for believing it was sabotage. It's why he always knew certain things.

"There's proof," he said. "The threads of the bits had been shredded—manually shredded, preventing their tightening." The random pattern of the shredding told him someone did it in a hurry while on the clock. Errors in factory tooling, which he'd seen before, didn't pick and choose their targets to destroy. They ran over parts uniformly. It wasn't enough to destroy them, though.

"Why sabotage?"

"Money. They make it with the skim as much as the drill.

Someone's been making a ton of it even during the shutdown."

Money fueled most motivations. If someone knew enough about the inner workings of the mine, they could control it. If they controlled it long enough, they could practically own it. They could milk it for its artisan diamond production, be content, and no one the wiser. He told me to think about how a little mouse could control an elephant.

"The clever can control the smart," I said.

"You're learning."

"Learning from the master."

He pointed to himself, not sure if it meant him. He laughed, thank god. I forgot he was one of us mortals. Now, that's my naivety speaking. I knew the talent and ability belonged to him, all the time. He simply deflected its ownership to ground him. It's humility. Something else plagued him, more profound than this place, or circumstance.

§

"So, how did they let you out?" I said.

His nose pointed to two blue camos, with big military jaws, sitting on the hood of a jeep.

"Chicotte let me out but only me. A part from South Africa's coming. Three days. The KEM's a concentration camp until."

He looked away. His gaze fell on Eden and stayed for a long time. When he turned back to me, his face floated by my frame, and the tent ruffled in the breeze behind him.

The meds kicked in, my gears shifted lower; and the drip of sleep came. As I dozed off, it came to me. "Wait. Mr. K. K., he did this to me, didn't he?"

Logos said yes, and although Chicotte had it out with the old man over the incident, nothing came of it. I was to stay away from him.

Eden slipped into view from behind him. "Robert, you should be right soon."

Logos asked her about the lines of refugees we saw while driving to the mine all those months ago. Where did they go?

They came to MAI, she said, the Red Cross, and dozens of other organizations. They treated the sickest, and sent them back out again, part of the Rwandan revolving door.

She sighed. "Triage central at MAI. We even treated the king's youngest daughter, Matilde, for a broken arm some weeks back, when she had fallen. The king was thankful, like nothing I expected. He came over personally." She looked away. "Remember, Angela?"

"Yes Mum." Angela nodded.

"It was a day," Eden said, taking a step back.

Logos urged us to appreciate what we had, and it sort of grounded us. Most people focused on what they *didn't* have, and it haunted them for their whole lives, deflecting them from what they *did* have. The focus made the difference between happiness and misery. His kitchen apron philosophy worked, again, always making sense in the cursive which embroidered the fabric of the mind. Man, it was perfect and killed me every time.

He looked at me. "Rest up for now."

"Right-o."

To my surprise, Logos told Chicotte he wouldn't begin until I recuperated. He didn't care about the prospects of the radio room-prison and doubted they would threaten him with it at this stage in the production. When I did recuperate, the excruciating work, and my fair share of it, would continue.

"Hell, part two," he said.

"Can't wait for the sequel." I raised the swaddled limb. "Still have my arm!"

"Right, Robbie." He tapped the tip of my nose. "One day, we're going to get off this rock." He said it like he almost believed it.

§

Angela propped a pillow under my head, and I caught Logos and Eden seated across from me.

He smiled, talked in a calm way. He touched her shoulder to make a point. She didn't mind. Her attention consumed a person, and he must've felt like the only other being on the planet. When her blue eyes opened, your heart skipped a beat, or stopped. They took it all in, and you fell in, and didn't want to ever return. Her eyes told what her ears heard. They welcomed and saw tomorrow coming as a better day. I wanted to be in his chair, be him, in the moment.

A dance of gestures developed between them. They handed them off to each other like two kids playing with geometric blocks, matching shape to hole on the other's board. Her energy overflowed at times, throwing her timing off. When it did, she contained it by sitting on her hands. She held them there until the energy settled, until she settled, and said something to make their pieces congruent in the game once more.

§

My body weighed down, so did my eyelids, and I fell asleep. I drifted away, so far away, I forgot from where I came.

I dreamt I floated in a dark chamber until I saw stars. A bulky suit covered me—an astronaut's suit. A tether made of real silver connected my suit to the craft's wall. I floated in outer space until gravity clenched my legs. It pulled me down into a black hole at the center of the spiraling galaxy. The tether pulled too. It morphed into a silver umbilical cord about to snap. My feet were being ripped from me. The force stretched me, *spaghettified* me, like the scientists said would happen at an event horizon. A nothingness swallowed everything up inside the swirling mass. My tether snapped. *No!*

In the center of the black hole were gigantic mirrors for walls. I was naked, shaking like crazy. I kept falling but into the mirrors. I didn't want to go. *Mom!* I saw the infinite and the nothing. A mass pulsed like a heart. The cold energy came into the spacesuit, sucking my breath away. I was besieged—even owned. It had a conscious. Something friendly? No. It was a fiend.

21
MASKS AND WIZARDS

I woke up squealing like an old gutter pup. My heart was racing, forehead dripping wet. I was back in the DRC, but never left, really, I only took a sojourn, a trip to the outer's outer, and back. I never thought I'd be happy to see this place again, but anything's better than being turned into spaghetti in the bowels of the Milky Way. The yelping became jitters, and the whole hospital probably thought this is the biggest wuss since wusses first came out of the womb. I couldn't relax, even with the breathing exercises I had learned to control the old rage.

The embarrassment had turned into shame. I always thought they appeared like different masks on Halloween. It was like this. Waking up, yelping, and being caught became the first mask, embarrassment. The second mask had built up over time, from the kidnapping, and long imprisonment, and made shame. Well, what was the difference? Embarrassment was public, shame, private.

Old Father Manso at VMA said shame was a secret, like being naked before God. Logos and I kept our shame to ourselves and from each other. But no one can keep a secret forever. After a few months, it ate away the organs more each day—and Lord knows you can't run from it. It resurfaces, wearing a dream as a mask, which you can't take off. Until we chose to tell an outsider what happened to us, the shame ate away our souls.

§

Things had quieted down. The hustle and bustle of medical business beneath the tent slowed, and those fussy doctors, beautiful nurses, and homely stretcher-carriers, all gone home by now. The sun had fallen, too, and the light ran like watercolor over the horizon.

My Angela brought me some water. "Doctor say we can lift your head." She placed another pillow there. "Why you sweat so?"

"A dream, I had a dream."

Everything looked bleached brighter, louder, and more irritating since I woke, except for her. The old vertigo did me like a top, too. I steadied myself by holding the jar of water. I sucked the water through a straw, until I heard the slurp. The old noggin adjusted, the body re-hydrated, and damn me all to hell, water *was* the cure-all here.

Angela kept moving around, tidying up, or something, but I couldn't be sure.

"You sweat, must be bad dream." She put her hands on my shoulder and lifted me some more. "Do not get too excited."

Too late, it was the most skin-to-skin entertainment I had in months.

"You be fine, sir. You trust doctors and Angela."

My angel peered at me from over her cherub cheeks. She looked like a TV star I always had a thing for, and in the nurse gown, she looked even better.

"You have one of those great faces," I said. "Really, like an angel."

I tried to convince her I was better looking without this contraption.

She weighed the image in her head. "I see. You have the nice eyes." She looked away, to the field. "They will call this, the romance under the tent."

They could call it whatever they wanted. I took her hand, squeezed it.

Angela turned back. She chuckled like a little girl, palm covering her mouth. She feigned wanting to pull her hand away from mine. She left it there long enough, supple, and accepting, like a woman's hand should be.

She tore it away, "Let me get back to work." Angela said she would return.

§

Propped on the pillows, I could see the world of the field hospital. Dozens of cots lined up like a barracks and made streets and avenues beneath the tent. Most of the beds were full and patients slept or stared at nothing.

The back of my head ached. I wasn't sure if it came from getting hit, or from when I fell, or both. About a million things snapped on and off inside my noggin like a strobe; all the work we'd done, and so much more to go. Hell, Part II, coming soon to a mine near you. The warm and heavies came and pulled me into sleep once more.

§

Before the kidnaps, and Kalashnikovs, someone passed me a business card at a party. It's how this snowball rolled down the hill, you could say. The soiree in the West Village was a sort of NYU graduation party. The run up to finals had been like some climb to Everest, and we could gradually begin the descent, brew in hand.

Around the same time, I ended a relationship with a girl—or she ended it with me. I like to call it my WTF era, the winter of '93. Comes in threes, they say: no job, no girl, family filed for bankruptcy. At the time, I had to contend with less money in my pocket—sure, but I lived alone in the dorm, and lapped it up, until Rose. I dated her before Lauren.

I met Rose in a West Side bar while on the prowl one night. Her eyes said she knew something I didn't, they said, *sparkle, sparkle*. It came from being older, more successful, two things I wasn't. She ran a line for one of the marquee fashion houses and never let anyone forget it. She was out of my league. I must've charmed her, though, as I moved into her postwar on east sixty-first street and lived it up. Soon after, the guilt of not paying my way grew into shame. I denied the obvious reality: Every man must shoulder their own obligations in this world. They don't go away, ever. Eventually, the infatuation came to an end like a good car wreck.

Infatuations have masks of their own. In the beginning, they require a blindness to see them through to their enjoyment, so you have to put a mask on. The other person knows it too, so they put on a mask. It's like being at a free masquerade party for two. But the bill always comes, and the embarrassment comes, and the shame comes, too, each with a mask of their own. It's why it's an infatuation.

By the time I graduated, my stipend took a crew cut. Out of respect, I didn't accept my parents' help anymore. I would have to earn my way. It wasn't a problem; I wasn't one of those lazy prick leeches—no way. For Rose, I saw it coming, the bill for the shelved obligations. She dumped me and my heart tumbled. I knew it, a man's got to provide for those around him, especially his woman. You can play blind, put a mask on, but the bill always comes.

Months later, I saw her on Lexington, walking all runway-like in her fur. As I passed her, she sort of raised her head. I thought she would say hello, but instead, she pursed her lips into a snooty half-smile.

§

This kind of crap bothered me less these days, especially when I compare it to what I'd been through in the last six months in the DRC, and the gladiator academy of VMA, and those bag of pricks, holy crap.

"Anger is angst's ugly cousin," the headmaster would say. "We must remove the pimple."

Villiers Military Academy was an all-boys school in Saint-Laurent which specialized in old school discipline. It's the kind of place you sent hardened future criminals when they reached the end of the line. If you're kid's a prick, a future Dillinger, Capone, or Berkowitz, stubborn as an ox, mad as a rattler, and you've had enough, send the runt our way. We'll fix 'em up right.

They exorcised anger out of a boy by marching, saluting, exercising, paddling rumps with a big Louisville Slugger paddle, and respecting officers, teachers, and those old guys made of Carrara marble in the yard.

The staff marched the halls in military garb, advanced degrees held in-hand like scepters. They told us when to study, eat, sleep, and shit. You accepted their edict, or got the paddle, or ten-miler march. I always chose the paddle—screw them. It freed up the afternoon for tennis or reading my old Playboys.

"Attrition, my boy," Father Manso would say in Anger Management. "Attrition is the great filer-down of sharp anger."

It was my sixth period class. After two years of getting my rump paddled—hey, I told them I was less angry. In time, I would become a productive member of *société*.

§

It was expensive to go there, but I knew money my whole life. At one time, my family owned the Bonhomme's Dry Cleaners chain in Montreal. You've seen them, or driven by, twenty-two locations, Bonhomme's For Every Home, the sign said. "We clean, seam, and ream you," Dad said, privately. We lost it all when new legislation forced my parents to shutter twenty of the stores. An atomic bomb hit us.

"Goddamn new rules," Dad would say. "They hurt the small businessman. It's a big transfer system."

It felt unfair. Today, I thought he was right, too.

§

Now, the NYU graduation party in the West Village. A former classmate brought me. He made out with a girl while a guy told me about a mechanic in Astoria who reigned over all things mechanical. I described to the guy my dilemma with my car. It spent a lifetime in storage, and I put my savings into resurrecting her.

He told me not to worry and handed me a card. A crease bisected *Wizard Engineering*. The next day, I checked my funds. I still had a few hundred saved, so I decided to take a chance.

The mechanic shop sat on the unfortunate flank of thirty-first street in Queens, in shadow most of the day from the elevated subway. It was dark inside the shop. A generator ran day and night. This wizard worked alone, no employees in sight. After he worked on the Porsche, we became friends. He asked me to review his job offer in Peru. He trusted me, or my education, or my naiveté, or something. My expensive education hadn't gone to waste, as I saw things in the deal he couldn't.

As I said, I can be a cynical bastard at times, and I like it about myself. It's gotten me into a bunch of problems with some things but is really good with others. In the print of the contract, he saw all the dollar signs, and zeroes, and a new life unfold. I noted a wicked clause or two which could eat away his pay. I got paid to sniff this out. He spoke with the people hiring him to get me hired as an assistant. After I signed up, I became the eternal optimist, and he, the crusty cynic.

§

A few months later, we met David from the Consortium. I'll never forget when they drove us to the offices to meet him. They said no one had seen this genius in three years.

"A giant above all other men," Ivan, David's assistant, said. "He's the only man with the vaccine."

David ran the entire African mining industry or had a hand in most operations. Men wanting to enter the trade, or needing favors, went to him on a pilgrimage, with offerings, hopes, and dreams of becoming rich, too. He was generosity, vision, and Bill Gates, in the flesh.

§

The old Lincoln idled in front of the offices, as Ivan listened to God himself on the phone. The same old prick who dropped us off at the airstrip, Tony, sat behind the wheel. His bobble-eyes filled the rearview mirror. Anyway, the gatehouse boom lifted, and we rolled in. At this point, everything seemed fine, except for the man with binoculars on the fourth floor.

A keypad cut out of a wall. Ivan punched in the golden code, and we went in, up the elevator, and into an office. The lights were dimmed. There were no chairs, or tables, or communal watercooler, only a desk. This "giant" was a little balding man, slight as a jockey. He sat at the desk. He wore a black suit, probably some custom-fitted import job, like we used to see at Dad's cleaners. A silk handkerchief hung like an orchid from his suit pocket.

"I'm David." It was the voice of a hypnotist. "We ever met before?"

"No," Logos said.

"I know everyone." David crinkled up his forehead. "Ivan briefed you. I'm an equity partner, here state-side to watch over things." A petrified smile pasted over his lips. "I can give you your signing bonuses." He patted his breast pocket.

Logos moved to the desk. He wanted to know about certain clauses in the contract.

"Boilerplate," David called it. "This has been thought about before you ever arrived. You'll share in our achievements, as our employee."

"I work for myself, my achievement," Logos said.

David had perfected an economy of movement, action without physicality. It emitted a quiet power, and put someone on the defensive, until they could divine its origin. He quoted Nietzsche.

Logos scoffed.

"Sorry to interrupt," Ivan said. "Logos, what's the problem?" He spread three fingers. "Three million dollars. *Probably*. Lot of dough. If we're successful, you'll make an additional percentage." A red band strapped a fastidious ponytail like a prized Maltese.

Logos pressed for additional upfront funds—the three hundred grand extra they eventually wired after we arrived on site.

To our surprise, David agreed.

I gave Logos the nod. The way I figured it, six hundred grand in the hand is better than three million in the unknown bush. I asked about the actual location of the job.

David looked at me for the first time, sending a shiver through me.

"People are sent where they're needed." He shifted back to Logos. "You read it. Today it's Peru." He handed us two checks. "You leave this week. First-class."

We thought it was a *few* weeks—no, everything had been moved up.

"The engineering plans?" Logos said. "Need to review them."

David waved off the question and unsheathed a pen. "Gentlemen, the releases."

We signed, and man, I thought we struck it rich. All my money problems, and my parents' home could be saved with the movement of a pen over paper. It was the biggest high of my life.

David showed us the unsigned Death Benefits Form, which he locked away with the rest of the documents. He handed Logos, *Building Mental Toughness,* in one palm, all sacrosanct. "It's the vaccine for the mind."

Logos took it.

"Oh, refer to our doctor for your shots. Typhoid, Hepatitis A, malaria, rabies, meningitis. Do it today."

§

Tony dropped us off outside the repair shop and sped away.

Logos stared into the trees. "Why rabies shots, specifically?"

I didn't understand. We were being offered a chance to dig ourselves out of our financial holes.

"Wild animals are rare inside a field camp," he said. We were missing something. We shouldn't get too comfortable, our guard could drop. A good opponent knows it. "It tells me we could get shipped anywhere without notice."

"But we have the money," I said. "It's proof enough."

He said we didn't have money, we had checks *promising* money. "Before a check clears, it's a promise. After it clears, it becomes money." He told me something which changed me forever: Don't see what you believe, believe what you see. He told me to remember it like the new Lord's Prayer.

Sure, always, I said. It threw me because Dad had always told me the same thing. Logos kept trying to teach me, this wasn't a game. We held our lives in our hands, and our decision would affect us forever. He hadn't told me everything, yet.

I had a hunch. "You some kind of operative?" I realized I'd begun to think like him.

He paused and it told me everything.

"During another lifetime." He winced a few times. "David thought I wouldn't catch this thing about rabies," he said to himself. "But I did. I'm tired." He walked inside, off in his own world, again.

§

I sat on a bench to think things through.

A couple crossed thirty-first bundled up like snowmen. They held plastic grocery bags, full, heavy, the sides splitting. A car sped up. It was going to clip them. *Walk faster.* It didn't make any sense. I thought I could make them move. Ridiculous—they couldn't know my thoughts. They made it to the other side, safe with the others on the sidewalk.

Thinking back on it now, I decided my future on the bench. I wouldn't let the old fear eat me up anymore. When I got home, I took action. I called Lauren and told her I was leaving Friday to go overseas.

"Hmm. Too bad." She chewed on something, pistachios she said, and apologized.

The truth is, I dreamed of maybe marrying her one day. I was one of those mushy committed guys you hear about. It seemed like another Robert, another time, now.

My stomach rumbled. "I'll think about you."

She took a deep breath. "You could work here, too." She was smart and quiet, and I never gave her credit. "It's what *you* want, ultimately." Her voice cracked. "I'll...um, keep a look out for you at the bank."

I'd make my fortune and come back and marry her. She'd see.

We laughed, and it became a mask for the tension over the line.

§

The deep sleep ended.

At the foot of my cot, Logos and Eden passed the time talking. They were in it deep.

22
EDEN

They leaned over an old desk, as if playing a board game. But there wasn't a board, or game, or any pieces to move between them. Each time their hands ran over the top, paint chips flaked off, and flapped over themselves like ticker tape.

For good ole me, it didn't matter much. I watched from the cot, playing the swaddled patient in a haze.

Eden tilted her chin back, shook her hair away from her eyes. "Your mum and dad? How did you get along?"

"My father, he um, left for weeks at a time." He became aware of the door into himself he was about to open. "He captained a cargo ship, so I was home alone all day. The whole only child syndrome."

Logos senior was a stern figure, half schoolmaster, half mystery, and coming and going from the front door like some actor in a play. He didn't say much to the young Logos. He nodded, dispensed his old captain's philosophy, and if someone crossed him, he did the old Mr. Hyde, too. His stare could intimidate the living hell out of anyone.

"I caught the brunt of it most of the time." Logos didn't elaborate and didn't want to keep the door to himself open anymore, not yet anyway.

"Hmm. Harsh existence. My mum worked for the Royal Navy. Family tradition 'n all. My father, too, before he passed away." She raised an eyebrow. "I always followed Mum. We were secretaries in Her Majesty's Service office. She stayed on for twenty years, 'til I finished university."

For both Eden and Logos, their parents drilled working-class values, but with Conservative Party thrift over spend, and responsible self-interest above all, as ethic. Those made their three meals per day; a lashing on the rump made dessert.

It sounded like the Bonhomme home after someone snitched me for the M-80 bomb put in the neighbor's mailbox. Man, you should've seen it blow sky-high. I got fourteen lashes on my birthday for it, too.

He looked directly at her. "What got you out here?"

A mischievous smirk came over her. "I split from a chap, plain and simple."

"You did something about it, though, rebels always do."

She crossed her arms, looked away. "I don't go around harping on my relationships." Her finger flicked the paint chips. She forced a smile. "Well, I wanted to be far away from him. Why not here, it's far enough? He was a bugger, y'know? The one you leave, and they find you to patch things up. I didn't want patching up anymore."

"You wanted something new?" he said.

"Yes, I said to myself, buy new."

Logos spotted it immediately. "Weld a bar over and over and it loses its tensile strength," he said. "You have to get a new bar."

Maybe everyone looked for it. People had to travel a long way to find the same things new again. The world made places farther away, yet people kept searching for the new.

"I'm here," she said. "It's my life now." A girlish energy filled her, one which saw tomorrow even better than today. "I've helped MAI with patients, dug holes, put up tents, cooked. I'm quite good, y'know? Yorkshire pudding's a specialty of mine, especially Toad in a Hole, which is Yorkshire pudding filled with little Brit sausages. I suggested it. They thought I meant putting an actual toad in it. Believe it?" She rolled her eyes. "So impressed with my culinary bravado." Her face turned flush.

The other patients woke up. Angela came over and wagged her finger at Eden. She gave a professional *shhhhh* right out of a textbook or something. She checked on me, and I sensed the old hop, skip, and jump in me. She waved good-bye.

Logos put off his usual dissecting, thank god. He did what Dad had taught me: listen when others are speaking, and you'll learn everything you need to know about them.

I saw it like tennis. My own scientific observations told me the person talking is usually on offense serving the ball, while a person listening, was setting up the return on defense. I kind of got it, and maybe the whole game was a little of both. Anyway, it's the first time I saw him adjusting to a long defense.

"Quite young when I split with him," she said, "and not so robust mentally. I had to be this far away."

What about the remoteness, the radical career change, her bare existence? It's no place for a beautiful woman to roam.

She insisted he would've found her, convinced her he was wrong, she was right, and she would love him again. It happened before, leaving her a wreck when it ended. She tired of the Friday pub scene, the same friends making dead-end plans, but only passed forward, or poured down throats like warm pints. They were all "frauds" because they spoke about action but never took it. She raised her pinkie finger, acting out a proper teatime.

I took it all in and got a minor in human relations. I've always been around adults, so I know a thing or two.

§

"How did you ever meet?" he said.

"Oh, god, office romance 'n all." She scoffed. "My first day at Reception, he sauntered in one morning at exactly nine a.m.. His Navy whites glowed, all groomed 'n shiny. He said: 'I have a nine o'clock.' My heart pounded away. I could hardly keep eye contact. This clock hung on the picture rail, and I looked there instead. Exactly nine a.m.. My god, I said to myself, this one's one to watch. Wilde said, 'Punctuality is the thief of time.' I don't agree. I like punctual people. I'm punctual, too. They don't lie to themselves the world isn't watching the time. Trust me, the world *is* watching. He introduced himself. I stared at his chin— it had a hole in it. It's all I could do. It had a dimple in the middle—a sexy one, though. It charmed me. For this young country girl, he seemed larger than life, like someone walking off the screen from one of those forties war films or something."

A kind of therapy developed. No crusty old doctor, appointment, or prescription was necessary, as the ear could heal the words coming from another's mouth. It helped clarify the past and them.

Eden felt lighter. She couldn't talk to anyone like this, especially all the way out here. She exhaled. "Love at first sight." She tapped the table. "Funny, isn't it? My rational mind tells me no, my heart says, yes. The first image of him branded me, you could say. The moment plays on and on. Oh, yes, it *was* love at first sight..."

Nothing compared with a first exposure, they said. The first crush, first kiss, first win—no *second* could ever top it. The rest of life was adjusting to the seconds, thirds, and Lord help us, the long fourths, and fifths. Most people thought the hard part of life was getting to the sweet spot, getting drunk, or fat, or worse, actually achieving your dreams, but no way man. Monotony made the highway of life, the divorces, drug abuse, career failures, and mid-life crises made the wrecks. No instructions came for this job, either.

They had solved the world's problems in one night. My god, a miracle. Call someone—United Nations, please take notice.

She declared a person's first love a spell. She shook her palms. "It's how a voodoo priest does it."

"They're sneaky."

"Diabolical."

"It's why they're voodoo priests." Logos kept a straight face.

The corner of her mouth crept open. "Quite funny when you want to be." She straightened up. "Now, one moment, *Mr.* Logos. You've hardly said a word. It's cloak 'n dagger. Spies do it to their potential targets."

"This target's fascinating to look at."

Eden folded her arms. "And you're a man full of secrets."

You should've seen him squirm like a kid in a barber's chair for the first time. The analytical, careful, all strategy man would be put under the microscope for dissection.

"I didn't plan this," he said. "I have the impossible to fix or the Ville dies." His voice cracked. "Too many stories."

"Would you tell me one?"

24
LOGOS

"What are you doing here, *exactly*?" she said.

"Working to save our lives." He flicked a nod my way.

I pretended to be asleep.

We were supposed to be somewhere else, same thing he told her when they first met, except everything crumbled. He told her the truth. He told her about the snatch job, the trip, the mine, the village, the radio room-prison, and good men, and their entire families forced to work, all wrought into slaves. We had told no one else.

She nearly fell over. "It's impossible. What will you do?"

"Get these drill bits installed. If not, the whole town might go down, including Robert and I." It weighed on him.

When he told me, a casual air came attached. Perhaps Logos didn't want to alarm me at the time, but his worry bled through now, and he made no attempt to stem it, along with the shame.

She surveyed the tent. "Are you still a hostage?"

He nodded at the two Congolese men with hard faces sitting on the hood of the jeep.

The men looked straight ahead and smoked. When they inhaled, the embers pulsed like dying stars out of the blackness.

"How did it all start?"

He explained the whole downward spiral of his life after Chile, the deal which broke his business, and the trip in the cargo plane which netted both of us. Looking back, it was easy to see, but what isn't in the rearview? He told her how we lived, how they treated the other men, how many went missing. He turned away from her for a moment. The shame poured out of him.

"Isn't it illegal?" She bent closer. "Why don't you run?"

He turned back. "At this point, I'm less afraid."

"You should be. I've heard things about them."

She didn't go into detail, but many had disappeared from the KEM. These were things she and the others at MAI heard about. No one could prove it.

He told her he'd been working on a plan. For now, he'd finish the work, as he outlined to me, and it would control the fear short-term. After, who knew? They might kill us anyway. He was worried but tried his best to control it. He sensed the sick aura which hovered over us as a permanent warden of body and soul.

The larger gloom which hung over us was the place itself. It surrounded us. If the plateau and KEM made a prison, the big land made the prison yard. The remoteness held people against their will, against escape, as much as chains, and guards, or the oppression of the bush. For others, the distance protected them from whomever they were running away from.

She didn't agree with him exactly but understood her own predicament.

"No police out here," Logos said. "Nothing."

She stood. "Who can I call?"

He held her wrist with two fingers going around like a bracelet, to sit back down. She didn't react. He left it there to test her. She let him and he let go.

§

Angela showed up with beer, cold, beaded on the sides. I wanted to guzzle one, but they weren't for me. She winked at Eden. Air kisses and waves flew between them, and Angela left.

Logos raised his beer to cheer, and they chinked their bottles. He nursed his bottle, dangling it by its neck.

The patter of busy feet trailed off. Crickets chirped.

She asked him, in real terms, was this slavery? It couldn't possibly exist in the modern world, and if so, he could get help.

It did exist, different only in name: forced labor, bonded labor, domestic labor, sex labor, child labor. At the KEM, hardship labor reigned and by default. Workers out of options survived any way they could. Men sold their labor to the only bidder in town, and got paid in cassava, mystery meat, water, and a hut. There was nothing more, nothing extra, nothing right, whatever in the hell *right* meant. Men did things to survive. If it meant forcing other men to become their tools and ATM machines, they would do it. For those with no options, it meant submission; look, listen, speak when spoken to, work, sleep, make stout shoulders, bow your head. You are part of the system, now. You are a machine. Bring your broken stick to the Master and submit. *Ump-thump, ump-thump, ump-thump.* You are a machine. This kind of slavery, see? It's the type of slavery we fell into. The type the men of the village fell into.

For us, the *privileged* labor, not much separated us from the Worker-class of men. In the beginning, before we ever left New York, we thought it was all about money. I finally got it, though. In this place, without your free will, money meant nothing. Survival was the currency for all men. The money had a price, but no real value, especially way out here. It couldn't buy your way out, or a burger, or even a compliment. We could run, but the mayor, police captain, and old Uncle Consortium would find us. Jando said it right: they always find you.

She didn't know what to say.

§

She'd hit a nerve in Logos, maybe the most tender one in the body. What would he do? Would he continue for the Workers or himself?

"My own work comes first," he said. "I'll attempt the install again. Someone tried to sabotage it before."

"How do you know?"

"There are facts," he said. "It's what I always go by."

She put her head to one side. It lay in her palm. "What about intuition?"

"Intuition is emotional, not factual."

She made a preparatory inhale, more than for breathing. She knew he thought differently—hell, we all knew it. But Eden discovered it now, and like old Columbus anchored on a new coast, she waited until safe enough to wade in. "How do you mean?"

He told her about the random pattern of the drill bit shredding.

She shook her head, sighed, strange things happen everywhere, she said.

They do, but he didn't buy into the world of the unexplained. The tampering occurred after we landed. When they brought the crates out to extract the bits, the day I became injured, the nail heads sat bent, and others were missing completely. On the plane, they sat flush in the pine, with all the red anti-tampering tape wrapping them like giant presents. These were facts, he said.

§

Her questions sort of cleared up our position. As things turned to crap, his tactics only escalated things. If he didn't lead the KEM to a positive outcome, someone might go bye-bye.

She wanted to know the meaning of his work.

"It's achievement, a quiet satisfaction. Makes me happy."

"Self-centered. What about generosity?"

If generosity made the person happy, it made it right, he said. Generosity shouldn't be pushed or forced by others. It should come naturally, and pressure to give made it coercion.

She crinkled up her forehead. "There's emotion, too, intuition, wishing, the feeling of hope. You aren't denying it, are you?"

He understood it, accepted it as part, and parcel of being born on this planet, and such. He didn't buy into it the way the rest of us did. The way he described it, emotion wasn't a form of cognition.

Wow. I wish old Father Manso could hear him.

"I don't wish, or hope, or pray—it's how I used to think. I have *convictions*. I base them on reason. Mysticism won't guide me or hold my hand."

Logos said, people sacrificed this life for reward in another. It happened all day, every day. They had no proof of it, but they would even sacrifice other people for it, all while forgetting *this* life. The mysticism of emotions, or faith, or even idolatry, he understood conceptually, but no, they didn't guide him. He needed proof.

"Our mind employs the most powerful tool ever given to a living organism: *reason*. It makes us superior. It's the tool we are given to survive."

She understood his angle better and so did I.

"When I look at the world, I see exactly what's there. A rock is a rock, red is red, as in the Law of Identity. From these perceptions, our reason forms concepts, and logic classifies the perceived objects. It's the way every person learns. Aristotle proposed it, but they destroyed his work in favor of mysticism. Religion sprang up to control the masses."

She asked him if it's how he intended to solve the drill connection, with reason.

He said yes.

Eden played a beautiful defense. She knew things, as he knew things, the source only different. She could see feeling. Their ideas clashed on the surface, and oddly, in time, complemented and fit. The people fit. Someone once said, relationships were like puzzles, people, the pieces, and some fit together better than others. That whole argument.

He told her about the men in the camp who were forced to hand in their broken sticks and become Workers. Sacrifice surrendered their minds and bodies to the Masters, or to the KEM, or Chicotte, or to every other thug which demanded it. We lost part of ours, too. Who were we kidding? We held onto the self-esteem part, which we buried so far down, only we could find it. The Masters could ask for it again, but it was worth injury to keep. He made me see it. He made me see I could put the old fear in a box and quantify it when something was worth protecting.

The hard streak in him showed up. "Without minds, men are lost. They're controlled, thrashed around." The words flew from his lips, hurried, staccato. "Without the tool, s...someone will devolve into a feral animal, the opposite of rational—" He looked away in self-reproach. "I—I'm sorry. I guess, it meant something to me."

She interlocked her fingers and made a chin rest. "Why are you this way?"

24
A BREAKTHROUGH

L ogos cradled his forehead in his palm.
    Eden watched him, not sure what to do. He came out of it, adrift, and if she hadn't reached out and grabbed his hand, he might've floated out into the void. No man comes to those steely life conclusions without them forged in a fire or two.

She encouraged him to keep talking. She knew something always made something else, one dot connected another, and wanted to know how.

"Your ideas, they're difficult to digest at first." Her hand ran across her face. "They make sense." She looked directly at him. "Why don't you *wish* or have *hope*?"

He hunched over as if shouldering a weight. He closed his eyes, scratched his chin. His attention pointed into the dark outside the tent.

She had to know. "What happened to you?"

Not a sound clicked under the tent; not a body stirred at this late hour. They became my world, and I, their most ardent fan.

He turned away. "My parents died in an accident."

"Oh, my god," she said. She sat still. "How?"

"An accident on the street." His head turned back to her. "No more about the past."

"I want to know," she said, standing her ground. If a breakthrough would come, it could only be now. Eden grabbed his hand.

He told her how he walked with his parents after school one day. He was ten, or eleven, or something. A bus exploded near the sidewalk and they were crushed. The torsos contorted into weird angles, legs, arms, broken branches. They died there, on the sidewalk. He didn't know a person could be moving and full of life in one moment, and lie motionless and vacant, in another. He swallowed his saliva.

"My god," she said.

He described what looked like a bomb going off. The shipping line his father worked for had been accused of transferring arms to the Middle East, and a journalist told his father he was being followed. Logos overheard his parents discussing it one night. He remembers them moving several times before it happened. There was never time to make friends or routines to keep.

"I thought, this isn't real," he said. "They would wake up—had to wake up." His father lay next to Logos's mother on the sidewalk. Logos tried waking him up. He couldn't.

As he told the story, the weight on him grew heavier, and his shoulders buckled.

"My father's dress socks fell to his ankles. So, I pulled his socks back up—to look normal. It's what a stupid little kid thinks. If his socks were pulled back up, he would wake up—be normal again. I thought, I could *will* him to wake up. It didn't work. So, I wished and prayed like a good Sunday school boy always did. Nothing. No will or wishing could do it."

He stayed next to them on the doorstep. He couldn't talk. He wrapped his arms around his knees and rocked himself. They took him to the hospital for a check-up, but he still couldn't talk. Eventually, they contacted his uncle in New York. He moved away with him.

"My Lord." She pulled him closer.

It's the way life forged convictions into us and made each person who they were. It's how someone became someone else.

"We can't will things to exist," he said. "We can't hope reality changes—no. *We* must change our reality." He saw things for what they were—fleeting, real only in the flicker of now.

"I see," she said. No more challenges came. She accepted this, him, for what it was.

"Do you remember them?"

Quiet, except for an owl conducting an orchestra of crickets.

He placed his rucksack on the table and removed the clock.

She tilted her head at it. "What's this?"

Every day he and his parents walked by a garage with a similar clock on the wall but made of wood. He wanted to make one from real parts. His mom bought them. His father took a few days off and watched him make it. He rushed to assemble them but his father stopped him.

"Do it slowly," his father had said. "Detailed work is what matters. The mind, if you let it, will lead the proper way. A unique piece should stand forever. This is a principle. A thing is weak, a principle is strong. One dies, the other lives forever."

"It's like a psalm," Eden said.

He hadn't thought about it for years, he said, until this very moment.

The clockface no longer kept the time. One hand hung down over the other, fixed at five-thirty, about the time he worked on the Land Rover in the morning. The bigger gear, which held the hands, looked intact. A hole remained where he had removed the smaller gear.

Eden looked into his eyes. "A very nice memento, but sad, if you don't mind me saying."

"It is," he said.

"Why am I right?" She made him think about it.

"The past is sad because it's gone," he said, looking away.

"No, Logos." Her will grew stronger than his. "Please look at me." He turned.

"The past is sad because we want to change it. I can't, you can't. We don't have the power. The space between *I want* and *I can't* is your pain."

He went silent. We saw a man implode. He shook his head, looked forward, forgot if it was today or tomorrow. Tears welt up. He got a grip, regained the old perky stare, and he came back to us, thank god. He replaced the clock into the pack.

They stood. He pulled her close. An overhang cast a shadow on them like a velvet blanket. Beneath the blanket, they found themselves, with the most direct form of communication, touch. His forearm slipped around her waist, her arms, around his neck. Her eyes closed and opened to see if it was him. His hands stayed ready, gentle, pulling her in, yet not too close, or too far, the right distance, the right height, the right touch, the right woman. He lifted her chin.

The lips met for the gentlest kiss in recorded time. They became one. In my mind, the two figures seemed to rise from the ground by the silver tether which appeared, drawing them away. His lips ran over her neck and bit the nape with gentle nibbles. They embraced; one body melded into the other; two forms became one in the shadow. Still, they floated. She looked into his brown eyes lost and found, all at once. He took Eden's hand, the rucksack in the other. They went away, toward the other side of the field. The invisible silver tether which kept him there, snapped, and they drifted, and she with him, vanishing into the night.

25
HOME SWEET HOME

What a night it had been. I didn't see Logos or Eden again for some time, or anyone I knew from before, only Angela.

A week later, my convalescence ended, and they let me go free as a bird. They said I was well enough to get back to work, and in fact, it *was* a temporary state of affairs, after all. My body could do the work of two men, but my one arm would need to work like two arms. Well, they packed me up, and shipped me back to camp.

I rode in the back of the jeep doing the old slip and slide around the bends and watching the starry sky roll by. Strange as this will sound, I was happy to be going back. I figured I couldn't spend my whole life beneath the big top, with the constant coddling, prodding, and petting of the old noggin to convince me I'd live again. I wanted to see the completion of our work over the past six months to make history.

§

Although relieved of my head brace, I needed my nurse and her kind of nursing. She assured me I would live, "You, fine and well, Mr. Robert. Well and fine. One day, if stars say yes, we see each other again." Could be, might be, the thought appealed to me, but I knew I'd never see her again. The time for it had past as another one of my infatuations. I enjoyed the ride and watched the stars pulse out of the felt sky like silver pinheads, *twinkle, twinkle*.

The two camos with heavy military jaws, which brought Logos

before, rode up-front, quiet, pensive, referring to me as their last chore of the day. Static squelched from the radios and they adjusted the volume. I hadn't seen the major prick guard, who thought he was royalty, for a while. People disappeared, showed up, more people came, and those old faces became these faces.

The air felt nice running over my face, through my arm's gauze wrapping. I regained mobility. I could move the arm around fine, with no sling attached. If I was a half man at one time, I was at least three-quarters, now. The arm felt god-awful hot beneath all the wrapping. Any time we stopped, the still heat came over us, wetting everything, including the layer beneath the gauze.

§

The high plateau of the mine rose near the second gatehouse. Strange lights emitted from its center, as if a movie premiere were in full swing. I waited for a ruckus to follow, as the bumpety-bump in the moonlight became too quiet. I figured it was the kind of quiet which always comes before the big rattle and awe. It never came. On the way, no one drove on the road; in the village, no lights, or fires to speak of. They'd set the curfew for eight p.m. for everyone.

As we got closer, the strange lights became spotlights piercing the sky from the center of the plateau. We stopped at the gatehouse. The guard on watch burrowed his head into the bend of his arm, fully asleep. The driver kicked him, and the two hard-faced guards laughed. I held out my injured arm beneath the lamppost, and I couldn't believe what I saw: the shadow bulged into a caveman's club, holy crap. The boom lifted and we drove in. They dropped me off near the headframe. I could walk back the rest of the way to my trailer. The lights drew me closer.

Six bright lamps on tripods formed a ring around the A-frame. Their beams shot into the atmosphere, electrocuting the huddled clouds. They lit up the mine and night became day in their circumference. The lights paid homage to the great headframe, and in the moment, became a temple. The air heated and thickened into a fog. It became hard to breathe. It was a hell of a sight, really, white-hot lights encircled an inert steel A-frame, turning night into day in the middle of a jungle, and not a soul around, either. Where was I? I thought someone flying in the clouds would see the same thing, understanding it as I couldn't.

The lights said, the temple waited, everything was in order, and all would be decided tomorrow. Logos had told me everything on the maintenance list operated now. I was satisfied, as it took everything out of us to reach this point. Some felt it more than others, but everyone paid in their own way. The young brown camo they tied up on the headframe as punishment disappeared months ago. Many others had disappeared, including Erik, and the Black Socrates.

§

Behind the headframe, a giant pill sat atop steel stilts for feet. It was the oblong diesel tank. It sat in the dark, as the lamppost had burned out. A tanker truck parked alongside it, filling it. It seemed odd at this time, as it usually delivered in the daytime. Perhaps Chicotte prepared early for the busy day coming. When the low clouds passed over the tank, and the spotlights bounced off them, short bursts of light beat like a strobe.

A superhero teen manned the fuel lines. He was tall and lean, and a long T-shirt hung behind him like a cape, with the sleeves knotted around his neck. The cape furrowed and flowed behind his neck in the breeze. He snapped the lines into the tank. A flashlight clicked on. He continued to work, turning the heavy valves on the truck, dispersing the fuel in a slushy rumble. The light clicked off and he looked around. When the light clicked on, Marc appeared holding the flashlight. He spoke with the driver. Marc's hands fluttered like butterflies, moving more than lips for talking ever could. He patted the teen on the shoulder, all friendly, and handed him a can of Coke. The driver checked the can's weight and approved. He made a bad impression of drinking from it. Both men craned their necks around. The driver handed him a small brown bag, and old Marc practically skated away with it.

§

I headed back to my trailer for the night. My caveman club itched, so I stopped to scratch it. I brought a twig along in case and inserted it from the wrist. I passed the spotlights, to the final path home. I liked the quiet of night and took my sweet time.

The light inside Marc's trailer was on. I thought to keep walking, but I stopped for some reason. I wish I hadn't. He sat at his desk, bare-chested, counting cash. I wanted to go even more than the night after I whipped his ass at chess. I put my head down, one foot ahead of the other toward my trailer.

"Robert, oh Robert!"

Marc waited in the middle of the path. His wrinkled polo shirt—the white one he always wore—shrunk over his hairy navel.

"How are you, my good man?" he said, all chipper. He claimed to be out for a stroll, but this wasn't an accident. "You look fine, fine, my man." He curled a few comma-smiles and aimed his chin at my club. "Could've been a catastrophic accident. I mean for the morale of all, the whole town." His polo shrunk up like a slinky and he pulled it down.

"It was, I almost lost my arm."

He shook his head, came to his senses. Well, sorry about all the insensitivity, sort of thing. It's what he really meant. His hand flapped it away.

I hoped he would pick up the cue: time for me to hit the sack.

He made an embracing smile, so long it could tie mankind in a knot. "You are well."

I played along. Maybe he could tell me something about what happened to me when I got injured. "Thanks for the concern." I asked if he saw Mr. K. K. do it.

"I stood downstairs with Chicotte, remember?" The pale hands rose, twisting into I don't knows, what's, and where's, as he may as well've been at Sunday Mass at the time. "I saw Logos leaning over the top rail when the loud noise came over." Realizing his hands twitched, he forced them down at his sides and became the old trophy we met on our first night's stroll.

I took a second to see if it rang true and it did. "They said Mr. K. K. did it."

"They? I don't know who *they* could be." He came closer. "It's as I said, Robert. But I wouldn't put anything past K. K. He's the type, you know?" He came close enough to smell me.

I didn't like it. "Type?"

Marc had an audience now, and he relished the attention of knowing something the rest of us didn't.

"The *vindictive* type," he said.

"He attacked me."

"Oh, I can empathize." He slowed his roll, salivated over the syllables like dessert. "Believe me. Odd, *odd* chap, that one."

His moment to shine, to enlighten the dim minds of youth which had fortuitously stumbled upon his classroom in the dense jungle, arrived. How lucky for me.

He lowered his head. "Some say the old narcissist can be vindictive."

"Huh?"

"Well K. K., sure, nothing to lose at this point. He's done all the war fronts, lost his family over and over, and now—well now, he's at the end. He's here." His hand swept through the black air. "This one has a protector. The bush is his home. Chicotte is his patron. There is time and space, and he waits for their right moment to—"

His face changed—an eyebrow raised, the other frowned. His lower jaw went slack. The coronas of his eyes inflated; the pupils dilated. He studied an inanimate object—me. His face looked gigantic and ugly when it approached mine. He made a feral grimace, a look an animal makes before an attack. It is cold, dead, and you are its object: the prey. The sinking feeling in the stomach wobbled me. The vulnerability of fear blinded thought. A cold sweat broke out. He knew it had an effect on me. In a snap, he dropped it all and returned to normal.

His gold specs pointed at me. "Do you *see,* Robert?" His tone turned sterile.

"I think so." I couldn't think straight. The fear blinded me.

"Good."

He relaxed. The spotlight, the control, still his. The bush seesawed.

"That look," I said. "I, I...fear it. It follows me..."

My pulse raced; blood coursed to my head. I saw a white screen where my thoughts should be.

Marc nodded, been down this road before, seen it a million times, you're in the right hands, sort of stuff. He had taken time to research it, thought about its nature. He guided me as a real teacher in the moment. For someone to harbor this sort of vindictiveness, he said, they'd need to be a narcissist. They can't empathize, and see the world as only good or bad, depending on their mood. They live in a paranoid world, where fear is the sky, anxiety, the ground. Deep within, they fear ridicule, being wrong, being less, or worse, being rejected. Oh, yes, he assured me. Vindictive anger comes from deep hurt, and they rage until they can make it right, until their little world is balanced again. There are the conventional, plain old vanilla-types, and the older, bolder, who couldn't-give-a-crap-types, too. They will stalk and lure their prey to unleash an attack. Revenge was likely their animalistic reaction to fear. They became violent because they couldn't understand or control it. Did I understand? Did I *see*?

"*Yes*. I see," I said. "But it's revenge against me!"

The schoolmaster stood by, all knowing, all understanding. "I heard you two had some sort of row before." He rung his hands. "Not my business. I've known him longer than you, however. He is a man who cannot control his violence. He is Mr. Narcissism—the vindictive type—this is K. K."

There were rumors Mr. K. K.'s family was slaughtered by the Force Publique, he said. During a village raid, when it was the Belgian Congo, they burned everything and everyone in retribution for the theft of cigarettes by a young K. K from a government shop. No one would ever speak of it after.

Come to think of it, I remember the old man telling us something about it while on the drive to the mine. Since, he always lingered, stooped, sat on his haunches, or trailed us. What was he doing? Aah, the teacher showed me. Yes, I see the light. Mr. K. K. pursued a quarry—me. A column of sweat ran down my spine.

Marc looked into the black sky. "He stalked you. He couldn't help it. There's no control. The difference between normal and him is control."

"Control..."

I breathed, focused, and controlled. My pulse slowed. My reason came back. I was balanced, again, at least for a moment.

He adjusted the specs back onto the bridge of his nose. When something bothered Marc, it became his tell. *What did he still conceal?* Perhaps Mr. K. K. wasn't necessarily like this stalker in purest form, he said, yet felt like a stalker, reacted like a stalker, but only he knew why.

I needed to rest, needed to lay my head down. This day might come to an end. "I should go." I walked away.

26

Marc stayed, not wanting class to end yet. Something still weighed on his conscious, plagued him even. The adjustment of his specs on the bridge of his nose said it. He cut a new path.

"You and I are friends," he said. "Let's not forget it."

Let him talk, I'll walk, and see where this goes. "Sure," I said, baiting him closer. I wanted to see what he might give up about the diesel tank exchange. My pulse slowed. I controlled it again. I'd never been able to control it twice in a row—wow.

He scuffed the soil, following me. "Robert, you walked by my window now." He prepared a pivot to something graver on his agenda. "I know what you might be thinking."

I feigned understanding. "*Good* friends don't judge." I let the old naïve Robert out to play; the little shit who boarded the cargo plane months ago wanting to see the world. "What are you talking about, exactly?"

He felt surer of himself and I let him. He needed to spin his late-night banking into something else. His new directness came with a design. He would bludgeon fact over the head and make it fiction.

"I was counting my own salary. It's how they pay me here." Better to acknowledge what happened, he must've thought. "I help some of the villagers with it." Then deflect it with a generous red herring, or upright charitable donation, or something.

His back straightened, self-conscious his hand was caught in the donation tray. What is it they always say to the tray collector? "Oops, I was only getting my change." The new design wasn't working its magic on me.

"You saw me doing something you're not sure how to classify. It's what I'm doing now—classifying."

I lost interest, needed to get going. I wanted to see if Logos was around.

Marc blocked my path forward. "Do you believe me?"

"Do *you* believe *you*?"

I let him go on. The more he talked, the more he buried himself. His late-night stroll at the diesel tank gave it away; the brown bag, empty Coke can, the cash, his nervous chatter, all facts which buried him.

I told him I didn't buy it.

He begged me to try and understand. His life had been sheer Hell here, the last decade, the road to it. Straight out of university, he traveled the world on a research grant from Imperial College. He graduated Summa Cum Laude, and like a debutante at their coming out party, everyone wanted a piece of him. When the Consortium plucked him out of the lab and hired him, he grew rich. He lived it up. He bought too much, drank too much, loved too much. It became easy—hell, expected from a simple boy from Tipperary and raised in London.

He learned as fast as money teaches. He liked the tables, the green baize of *00,* and spin of the wheel. He made and lost small fortunes afterwards all over Europe. He abandoned his work, and worse, forgot where he came from. Late one night, in the dim and smoke of the Monte Carlo Casino, while sipping Louis XIII cognac, someone whispered to him the riddle of the mine: How could one make a small fortune mining diamonds in Africa? Start with a large one, they said. Jansen Pretorius had cornered him in one of the private high-roller rooms. He advised Marc to come back to work. The Consortium needed him, he said. Marc didn't listen.

He went on in search of his God-given place in this world. He would find it: debt, divorces, the Anne he never found, a short bout with mistress heroin, and a decade past. It stamped his golden age as: *Done.* The slow tangled climb to old glory began at the KEM. Pretorius eventually recruited him back for David, gave him a title, too: Head of Exploration, Kivu Equatorial Mine, KEM. It didn't mean shit. In Marc's case, the start signaled the end.

The KEM wasn't a bad place to begin one's career two decades ago. The old hole still produced. One could, as Dad always said, find the top and get out, while the others still thought they were on the upslope.

These days, without someone like Logos here doing mechanical CPR, they put those geologist-prospectors out here to graze. It's a long, long way back to Tipperary.

§

"You don't know what I've gone through to survive out here," he said. He gave me the skinny: "Year after year of being shut down, dealing with everyone here. The heat, rain, loneliness—everything." He couldn't take it anymore. He talked about the damn war which kept spilling over here. He mentioned it like his recurring back ache from the cricket days: Ibuprofen would do, sonny boy. That kind of thing. "It's caused problems—oh, surely." Now, with the curfew, no one could even leave the gates. It was unbearable for a man of his stature, a man of his pedigree, his *provenance*, even. He begged me to understand, empathize, at least. "I've had to squeeze out a living—as your boy Logos deftly put it. To survive, to survive, it's anyone's goal, isn't it?" A desperate sweat wrapped him like cellophane. "There are things men need to do. It's simple. I don't have anything else. No one can make this place any better, either. Logos can't." He pulled down on the polo shirt. His hand shook. He pivoted and reset, back to Marc one point zero, all over again. "Now, Robert, I can make it worth your while."

Now that whole thing hung over. It hung lower and darker than the clouds over the A-frame only thirty minutes past.

I didn't need to think about it. "No thanks, Marc."

He smiled all toothy and yellow and gave me the old "rubbish."

I kept my mouth shut.

He said there were others here which did a similar thing—but not him. He wouldn't name them and wouldn't admit to anything. By the way, the proceeds of the stones went to help others—not him, never, ever. If altruism had a face, he said, my god, it was his. "We'll leave it there."

He told me something which straight-up shocked and awed me.

"Robert, you're an honorable man."

Goddamnit. He said it to mindfuck me. He wanted me to place myself up there on some pedestal with those kinds of guys, and he would be the one holding the ladder. He could make me his accomplice by the shame of self-imposed guilt. His hand thrust out to shake.

I didn't want to. "Good night." I walked down the path.

"Let you win at chess," he yelled.

He squeezed a snooty smile at me. The same "goodbye forever" smile Rose made on Lexington after she broke it off with me. God how I hated it. "Bullshit!"

He stood there, keenly aware someone other than Logos saw through him. Something told me he may've sabotaged the twister plate to keep his side business going. There was no way to tell but I had a hunch. If his nervous tell was pushing the bridge of his specs back up, his desperate tell came in the form of sweat appearing like cellophane. If so, it told me the skim is how he made his real money. The skim made money as much as the drill, for those clever few. I needed to find Logos and tell him.

27
FEAR CONTROL

Although Marc surprised me with his cheap offer to buy my silence, I was more surprised at my reaction to it. I wasn't easily thrown off this time. I kept the angry dungeon of my mind in check for a moment longer, the fear contained to a degree, and the old rage from rearing its ugly head. It wasn't complete, or full proof, but man, I made progress. Like the chess game, I could see the moves coming, but as far as controlling the emotions for any sustained time, I couldn't do it. When I could see the moves coming, I sensed reason and saw it as shafts of light coming through a dense cover. It lasted a few seconds and gave me a power I had never felt before—control.

§

A front came through, leaving the smell of coming rain, and still, I took my time walking back to the trailer. I loved the smell.

The week away felt longer, and the old and familiar looked new again on the path. The grime on the white trailers dripped more. The old dents cut deeper. The bush grew thicker over the pathway, clawing back its possession. Two guards stood outside our door, one asleep, the other too awake. Their faces shined silver in the moonlight.

Inside the trailer, the thick mustiness wafted out. We had become used to the scents, dents, and grime, and the screams at night, which jolted us out of our beds. A few times, Workers were taken kicking and screaming by Masters down the path into the darkness. We saw them through the blinds. Sometimes we woke in the middle of the night, and the screams we heard were our own.

§

Logos snored away. I wanted to shake him awake and tell him about Marc. Look. I made it back. I'm in one piece, and could work again, although limited. His mouth crept open, hand outstretched over the side of the bed. I left him alone, no time for the old chinwag. Sleep brother, if anyone deserved a bit of shuteye it's you. I was beat too. The past week turned out harder than we imagined; one of the hardest of my life. Crap, I almost died. Little bed, where are you? All I wanted was to lie down for a lifetime, forget it all, and wake-up a new Robert, in a new place, far, far away. It didn't happen.

The beam of Logos's flashlight twisted over *Building Mental Toughness*. I picked it up and read. He dog-eared the chapter "Fear Control." It stressed the brain's emotional center, the amygdala, needed to be kept under control. Yes, emotions originated in the mind, first, not the old pumper in your chest. If the amygdala couldn't be controlled, someone could react with instinctual animal programming, overrunning reason. Logos underlined it. It sounded like something out of one of my VMA Anger Management classes.

In a panic, long inhaling, and exhaling produced a calm state. Maintaining it longer term, required the more advanced techniques of visualization and goal setting. These created short-term milestones as "distractions," to calm the amygdala. Logos mentioned it before, not so technical, not so scary. Balance was the key—the control. A quiet amygdala returned reason—the vaccine for the mind.

The key—I'd found it. If I could control the old fear, the rational mind would return. I could hold the reigns of reason at will. They worked together. I saw the connection, finally.

I put the book down, lay down, as the long day did me in, but the goddamn mattress was missing. I had to lay down on the wood bedframe like some old corpse. I couldn't believe these pricks. Oh, well, I was too tired to care. The warm and heavies came, and I felt tied down, as if by countless strings held by Lilliputians. *Rest, my boy, rest until tomorrow...*

§

Logos shook me awake. In the first light, he looked unsteady, like a drunkard woken up too soon. I knew he never touched the stuff. He simply looked older, walking dead tired, even in the dawn. He stumbled back to his bed and fell face first.

"Today's the day," he mumbled.

I hoped they would've postponed it, to recuperate some more, but it's life at the KEM. They dictate the terms, you walk rank and file over the cliff. I told him what happened after he left the hospital. For now, I was better, could work some. I would do my part.

He gave me the onceover. The part from South Africa came, he said, and everything was prepped. The people waited, and Chicotte arranged some grand inaugural party, where the whole territory was being bused in.

I asked about the night with Eden.

A precocious smile bled through his lips. She lit something inside him, charged his battery, and tomorrow would be a better day, silver lining and all. He took a few deep breaths and came around.

"You look brand new," he said, giving a thumbs up from across the trailer. "Straight out of the factory." He overflowed with energy, and I hadn't seen him this way since before we ended up on this rock.

I didn't exactly feel factory new, only rested, and better than him, for sure.

The lines of his face sunk deeper, the eyes darker, the cheeks hollower. His skin had tanned into brittle saddle leather. Before these pricks shanghaied us, we had the same milky complexion. Since landing on this rock, he was always baking in the sun, or pounding away on a dinosaur, or lost inside the guts of a generator. Even while I was away, they pressed him to hand over his broken stick, again, and he told them no. It meant more baking, longer hours, less rations, cots with no mattresses, and harangues from the Masters—but screw them. He was able to do the work of a dozen men. Still, they always needed more. On rural Ontario farms, they whip the stronger draft horse even on the verge of collapse to get the last drop out. I guess he was the draft horse, the king, the farm owner, Chicotte, the whip. Mr. K. K.—who in the hell knew?

I couldn't figure out what I represented, but looking at my gauzed arm, I laughed at the prospect. "Look." I lifted it up. "Got a caveman's club."

"A bundle," he said, twisting up his forehead. His mind focused on something else. "You got a bundle of cash, too." He hid something, the short smile, the wrapping paper.

"Eh?" Holy crap, what's he talking about?

He told me he argued with Chicotte about me not getting paid. When nothing came of it, he made the transfer into my account. He came over to the side of my bed.

"One hundred fifty k." He put his hand on my shoulder. "You deserve it."

Son of a bitch. I couldn't believe it. Except for my parents, no one had ever done something like this for me. Good thing I was laying down, otherwise the old caveman would've fallen down.

"I...uh...um." My throat tensed up. "I wanted to live up to my promise. All the 'I want to make history' crap."

He scoffed. "I thought I had an ego." He sat at the table. "You take the cake, my man. You've matured, too. Four months ago, you were young and dumb. A beginner."

"Thanks, I think." I was speechless.

28
A GOOD DAY FOR A REVOLUTION

Whew. So many things went through my old noggin: everything these pricks did to us, the survival we shared, the money, the genius criminals I read about, the mention of freedom by Chicotte—real or not. Maybe we had a chance for a life after.

Logos crossed his arms. "Like I said, you deserve it. And according to you, you're my only friend."

"You've got plenty."

"Not true, Robert."

"You're right, it's not."

I still couldn't believe what he did for me. I hid my face, choked up.

He stood. "We need to begin."

I stood, too. I mentioned Marc, and the possible sabotage, and how I connected it. I had thought about it long and hard. I went through his process, making it my own.

"Oh?" Logos's eyes narrowed.

I told him about the exchange at the diesel tank. I saw things for what they were, not what Marc wanted me to see. He probably damaged the twister plate for the drill bits to keep his skim going.

"The last part's not certain," Logos said. "Although I wouldn't put it past him. Your perception's sharper."

He looked out to the path outside our window. The window shade had gone missing, and the soil cover reflected into the room, painting it red. The guards watched from across the path, far enough not to hear. He said they all steal to survive out here. The Consortium already knew.

They didn't crack down on management doing it to keep them happy. After all, who came way the hell out here *not* to get something extra? The Consortium would make it all back a million times. It's why they paid him what he demanded.

He said our aim was to shoot higher. Our work would create wealth and a new way of life here. The achievement would change the thinking in people. It would change this place.

I shrugged.

Instead of *us,* he spoke about *them* more—those guys living where the smoke corkscrewed out of thatch roofs. If they joined our side it would help us.

What in the hell, now? The captain had changed our tacking. Ready about.

He put it this way: we couldn't get ourselves out, but the Workers could rise up, as a revolt against the Masters, and give us cover—a sliver—to bolt out of there. It's where the old Land Rover came into play. He'd thought about it longer and harder than he led on. He said he spotted a weakness in the fence line, in the vicinity of the radio room-prison. The plan was sketchy, but if the camos were drawn away, and we could drive the Land Rover, with a couple of tools, and a few minutes, we could breech the fence.

I wasn't ready to congratulate him. Escaping during a revolt seemed like the easy part. The harder part was, how did someone spark the *actual* revolt? It wasn't something you pulled out of your back pocket. Although the spark was harder to come by than the flame, all his years spent in South America doing the unimaginable, may not have gone to waste.

He spun the more complex part of the plan. The men were ready, as Izbart had told him in private. They only needed a nudge, and we could help them fight for their freedom, and in the process, help ourselves. It would rid them of the collective. No one could say when the fire might ignite the gasoline, and if it would burn big enough and long enough. One thing was sure, this agent provocateur held the matches.

He kept pushing the timing—today was a good day for a revolution. He would gauge the men's reactions to be sure. Those genius criminals in the paperback novel would've never come up with this. Although they thought two moves ahead, they never thought four or five moves ahead, the way Logos did. There was more to it, sure. When it came to Logos, it was always in the details. He didn't want to tell me everything, but I had to trust the guy.

"I thought we were trying to get the hell out of here alive?" I said. "Now you're talking about changing this place."

He did an odd thing. He looked down the path, in the direction of the headframe. Something told me, mentally, he was already there. He stood on top of the A-frame, hands dug into the grime, planning the spark of revolution. He saw it as changing the world. He kept saying, he wanted to leave something behind. It sounded like his dad talking; the one from the other night. Yes, we were doing this for ourselves, first and always, but it could help the men, too.

I stepped closer to him. "How about me? I want to live."

"I said I'll make history, and I will. Maybe it gets us out, too."

This wasn't two birds and one stone, anymore. It was two grown men, a village, all Eastern Kivu, and my own dear life.

§

The new grand scheme was another one of his calculations. He got into some of the plan, and it went something like this: if men thought for themselves, they would stop thinking as slaves. We knew the word had spread already, and Izbart led on there was an appetite for more. Workers, and even Masters, might fight for their share, to become independent traders, men without shackles, or fear. In the middle of the rout, our one and only chance would come, with the Land Rover waiting as a limo. Tinder-spark-flame—he said it would be a capitalist revolution—an inferno—first one in Africa. History 101—sign-up for it now.

Oh crap. He talked like my dad, and I understood better. He had a plan to bring royalty to its knees.

"These fucks put them under the boot," he said.

I imagined King Ulindi's big cane pressed against the small businessman's cheek. I saw it pressed on Jando, and his dad, and every other father, son, mother, and daughter panning the sludge. *Cane and boot—to hell with you.* Logos, or Dad, wouldn't stand for it, and neither would I. If we could help ourselves, and help the Workers in the process, I was in.

"Damn right," I said. "My dad says each man should be an independent trader. They keep this world running." The KEM was a fiefdom which enslaved men by enslaving their minds first. This land,

and others like it, were estates which us serfs tended for the lords. The lords tended it for the king. "Dethrone royalty who doesn't produce!" It sounded like my dad walked into the room.

Logos came up to my face but looked through me to a place only he knew. "Dethrone royalty." He took a long breath, grounding himself, as the chapter from his book recommended. "The work begins now."

"Yes, sir."

What was the actual plan? How to spark a fire without a match?

It was better I didn't know any more, he said. Simply put, one mind could act like a match sparking the others into a bonfire. He held the first match; tinder-spark-flame.

The ticking in my chest revved back up. We were playing with nothing to lose, again. Here we go.

§

He put on his black jumpsuit; the same one he had on when we got inside the goddamn Lincoln which took us to the airstrip. He took his rucksack and walked out.

I took off after him but I forgot my boots. I found them, slipped them on, jogged after him. He was down the path, to Main Street.

When I caught up to him, a full-blown carnival had sprung up. Women carried children, and children carried flowers, and everyone cheered. Men sat atop the shoulders of other men, all singing and dancing. The crowd grew into a drunken carnival, moving and breathing like a new species.

29

THE MARCH

A dozen camos waited for us in a file. They told us to march in the middle. Blue camos marched in front, brown camos, behind. Each man's legs moved in sync with the blue camo leading up front. Our legs lifted and fell, and we couldn't see the ground. My heart ticked, breath clipped, as we got closer. Logos followed them, and I followed Logos, and what may come, may come. There was nothing else.

Our file opened a wedge in the dense carnival which gathered around. The crowd grew, with more on the outside, and people trying to break through to the inside. It grew restless and changed again, into a mob. As our file moved forward, the mob split sideways, frothing up like seawater against the hull of a ship. Hands came into our procession wanting to touch us. They followed Logos and wanted him most of all. He shook hands, waved, but never stopped moving forward in the rush. He glanced at me to see where we were, where we came from, and where we were going. He pat me on the shoulder, and I would remember this moment forever.

§

Our procession was holed up inside a howling mass. Thousands had swarmed in from all over the territory for general admission. Some villagers ran toward the crowd's dense center, others strolled in large cliques, wide-eyed, cheery, expecting a life altering event, or show, or some other temple inauguration where the money would flow. Women carried big flower baskets, and some of the flowers fell, and baked into the red clay.

The mass, realizing our direction, shifted toward the headframe. They moved us along, and we moved them along. They were a river, and we were a river, and they flowed into us, and we flowed into them. There were bodies and heads and colorful garments and dashikis and headwraps and good scents and bad, and more flowers. Mystery meats on sticks raised up from the center like posters at a rally. Straw hats made face fans. Shirts rolled up into sweatbands. The hoots, the hollers—my god. A merciful breeze, a reprieve from the heat and chaos. Thousands of feet sifted the soil cover, sending it up into a persistent red cloud.

The world gathered around the headframe. They made taut concentric circles, the more important, on the inside rings, and the rest according to their caste. At the center, King Ulindi looked regal in an orange dashiki, with matching kofia cap, and holding the old cane.

The button-down-shirted men came next, pulled closer to him like metal filings to a magnet. When they could, they tried to touch him, or shake his hand. Their wives, or companions, held bright fans which fluttered at their wrists. The men sweated through their shirts.

Everyone got as close to the king as his security would allow. They pushed back those who didn't belong, those who were from another ring. Chicotte oversaw it. He had on his best military garb; war metals hanging, leather belts crisscrossing, shiny, shiny boots. A red fez made a top hat.

In the next ring, the voluptuous woman surrounded herself with a mini female court of her own. Her head rose above them; her eyes set downward. Soft drums beat. Voices hushed around her. When all stepped away, some ritual twitched on, and her body changed.

It was her but not her. Short white stripes below her eyes painted bones, with more stripes across her jowls. An artificial exoskeleton connected a web of stripes on the arms, waist, and legs. They had painted the dead on her. A necklace made of crocodile teeth scratched at her sternum whenever she shifted. It looked exactly like the one Mr. K. K. wore on the plane. The rest of the women dressed in bright yellow frocks, matching like a cheerleader squad. The hues clashed against the blue and brown camo of the security troops in the ring next to them.

The camos moved and clicked at anyone coming too close. They pushed back against the Workers. The hardhats were being pushed by hundreds of artisan miners in their T-shirts, shorts, and sandals. Each group made a ring of their own.

The mob controlled the final ring: stragglers, spectators, looky-loos, untouchables of the gutter, the gaunt, the injured, the glazed-faced, high-boned, high-browed, bare-chested, bare heads smoking darts, missing teeth, fingers, or limbs, and boiling in their Afros. They fanned out like tiny shards fallen from a larger mother boulder. Each man pushed and conspired to get closer to the center. In between the fits of shoving, the festive outer ring sang, broke out into dance solos, hooted, and hollered.

A solitary man, something more wire than flesh, crouched, and cried with abandon, arms shot to the sky. All rushed past to see better. Children sat atop the shoulders of men who sat atop the shoulders of other men. The carnival seesawed.

§

The massive footing of the A-frame clawed into the soil like a talon. We marched there, and to the stairs, which would eventually take us to the top of the temple.

Oohs and ahhs rushed over the heads of the crowd. A head pushed its way through the rings, into our file. It was a familiar face—the Black Socrates. He had become a stick of a man and could barely stand. A white bandage covered one side of his face. He had two distinct sides now: black-white, like a man being split apart. One eye moved frenetically doing the work for two. He fell to his knees when he saw Logos.

"T-the reason of the mine," he slurred over the rabble. "The...the reason of—"

A brown camo pushed him back into the mass of heads, and I never saw him again. Logos shot me an uneasy glance. It told me if he sparked a fire, Uncle Kalashnikov could put it out. Life would come down to a few moments. We pushed on.

The human train rounded the A-frame footing. They made us part of the entertainment, a troop parading in front of the officers like some real French Foreign Legion on graduation day. Our little troop marched in front of Marc, Chicotte, David in an odd golfing cap, King Ulindi and his witch doctor advisors, Mr. K. K., the voluptuous woman, and several button-down-shirted men.

In the hard light, David looked slighter. His presence felt even more out of place than his outfit. He inhabited the civil office world I once knew growing up, not the dirty field of now, and here, and who we became. We were no longer the strangers in this place—he was. He hardly moved his head except for down or up. He shared an exchange with Logos, a recognition of the other's existence, but nothing more. Someone eventually handed him a hardhat. A man took a picture of them, but David stepped out of the shot before he could snap it. He waited until the photographer left before showing his face again.

We halted under the headframe.

§

Mr. K. K. was there. I hadn't seen him since he injured me. I needed to stare at him in the face. I refused to look away like some kid crapping about what hid behind the door. It had to be done, and I had to do it alone.

He stood behind Chicotte. I summoned up every bit of will in me and threw a look at the old man. He stretched his neck the other way, knowing I was there. I didn't break. I surprised myself with my deliberate gaze. I was gaining control.

He turned his head back around like some Terminator taking in the scene. I saw a face but no man behind it. The spark of life went with it, leaving only flesh, and cloth, and his skeleton as a hanger, behind.

I could've killed him, mind you. I imagined picking up a squared-off rock and slamming it against his head. He fell over, moaned, and stared at me to confirm my victory. They all knew he deserved it, retribution—signed, sealed, delivered, goodbye. *Say hello to the new bye-bye man. Come to me if you want to go bye-bye.* I lost the control, again.

It's what my parents, counselors—heck, even close friends saw coming. Unchecked anger devolved into violence. It started in youth as angst and grew like a weed into fear and anger. Shaken together, a cocktail of violence was poured out. So, it was no goddamn accident when they transferred me to VMA for the major attitude adjustment—hell, I needed it. They said VMA's where the beast became a man. Each of us abided its rules, for rules made a discipline, and a discipline made physical punishment. Without discipline, things went unchecked, anger reigned free. It's what happened to people way out here. The remoteness—the void—changed a man. One thing made another, one thing led to another; the decline couldn't be stopped. I couldn't be stopped.

I became a colossus, again, as on the cargo plane, and everything ahead of me would be annihilated. My reason was lost, and the world shook when I walked, and the world, and him would pay. Every bastard would pay. *God damn it!* I might get my chance to say bye-bye.

30

T wo white vans pulled into the lot behind the crowd. Eden, Dr. Ramirez, and two Congolese men came out. They walked toward us.

Eden looked beautiful. Her blond hair set back, her blue eyes set in, soft, vigilant. Her face, simple, clean, and more interesting to look at each time. I've seen women's faces which appear stunning at first, but the novelty always wore off. Her face turned into a discovery. The more one looked, the more features could be found. They grew countless for someone who could see the difference between the stunning and natural. Logos looked at her, discovering it.

A whistle blared from the front of the file drowning out everything like an explosion. We were forced to stop. The blue camo pointed for us to go at ease and the march broke up. Logos walked over to Eden and placed his hand out. She took it, held it tight. An ease had developed between them. He told her she looked wonderful. She creased up her forehead, shot her hand over her T-shirt, her unmade face. It made no difference. I could tell he wanted to kiss her. She wanted him to kiss her, but another time, and place.

Dr. Ramirez jerked his head back.

"Thanks for coming, Lady Rebel," Logos said.

She stayed still and modest. "I wouldn't have missed it. They sent some chaperones for the event." She looked over at the good doctor, and the other men from the hospital.

Logos was happy she came, chaperones, or not.

She thought for a moment. "This Lady Rebel's happy to be here."

"Haven't stopped thinking about you."

"Well, well, you've been on my mind," she said, lighting up.

He squeezed her hand. We had to go, he said. The ceremony, launch, the holy install waited for us. He shrugged and she understood.

She wrinkled up the corners of her eyes at the painted voluptuous woman.

He shrugged again. He promised Eden he'd see her later and took a half-step away.

She held on to his hand. "Fine." Eden watched Logos walk on.

§

The distinct rings of the mass broke up, jumbling hardhats, spectators, and even parts of the king's court.

Logos stood with arms hung down, one hand clasped over the back of the other, across his waist. The blue camo guards stood behind us with their hands in the same position, same time, at five thirty. One of the men gave a slight nod to him, and Logos nodded back. Maybe Logos's insight into the minds of the men wasn't so farfetched.

Chicotte stood before Logos. He folded his arms, rocked on his heels, this African Mussolini in fez, sure to make his warning to Logos not to fail, come across. He stepped to the side for King Ulindi, who pumped his bony finger to the top, five stories up, where we were going like it or not. He spread his arm out for the voluptuous woman to come forward.

Drums pounded from within the mass, and the inner ring clapped in time with the drums. The voluptuous woman's head rolled about the crowd as if hung on a thread. Her torso bent nearly parallel to the ground. Her bare feet stamped the red dust, stepping on sharp rocks without flinching. Her body convulsed. One hand went behind her head, the other stretched out straight, as her legs shuffled her body around in a figure eight pattern.

The king conducted her trance, his bony index finger, the conductor's stick. He watched the crowd react to her heaving, swirling, the perspiration dripping on her neck. Her looped earrings spun like hula hoops. King Ulindi looked at the crowd—no, he *studied* the crowd. As the woman's hand rose, the crowd breathed in deeper. When she spun, their lungs exhaled in lockstep to hers. He conducted her to play the crowd.

Six females from her court joined in at her side. They mimicked her manèges, allegros, grand jetés, all contorted, or cut, or bent. They made clumsy muted pirouettes of their own. The voluptuous woman spun faster, feet thrusting the red dust into the mist outside the barbed wire fence. She ran one hand over the crocodile necklace, while her other hand pointed up, shaking. How it shook. The other women joined hands around her, scampering counterclockwise, heads flipping up, down, up, down, up. The horde burst into cheers. The show had begun.

§

They were advancing the ceremony, and by way, the crowd, to some dramatic point only they knew about. It had been done before, only we were watching now, part of it, or because of it, and there in its midst.

Marc watched us watch the dancers. He took pleasure in watching us figure out what was happening. Although distant at times, a wry smile came over his face. His eyes pointed for me to see Mr. K. K., who fell into a trance of his own, from the woman spinning...spinning...spinning.

King Ulindi lifted his hand—stopping the dancers. The voluptuous woman dragged herself to the king. She whispered something into his ear, turned, and shot a wicked glare at Logos. We didn't know what to make of it. The king motioned for Logos to come before him, and all the other management pricks, which stood by like an impromptu tribunal.

I looked to where we would climb. Izbart waved to me from the top floor of the A-frame. He paced, anxious for us to climb the stairs to begin the work alongside him. Jando stood next to him, and his hardhat kept falling over his eyes. Izbart tapped his heart, gave a thumbs up. I waved back with my head.

Chicotte jumped on the stairway, using it as a rostrum. He swallowed a massive breath. "Here is the *great* man we spoke of to help us move forward. Go up. Make us rich again!"

31

The request struck like a mortar, leaving shellshock and confusion over the crowd, guards, Workers, and other Masters. No one had ever called a laborer, or a Worker, "great" since any one of them could remember. They all looked at each other.

"Me?" Logos said.

Chicotte kept a straight face, solemn as anyone leading a funeral procession. The machine inside him, which plucked emotions on demand, went to work, and I imagined it pulling his lips apart by thin wires to speak.

"You are him," he said. He tried to hug Logos, but it wasn't honest, or true, only slick, and ugly, and what a crafty politician would do on election day. He smiled big and bright to them, grim when facing us. "We wish you luck before you go up." He pointed to the metal stairs.

The king nodded his approval to Chicotte, David, and Marc. All nodded back as a unit.

Logos looked straight ahead. "No luck necessary," he said. "I use reason." He walked, thought, talked at his own pace. Nothing swayed or coerced him away from it.

Applause erupted from the crowd. Real fans moved in their ranks, making their presence known in bits and pieces. Many of the guards whispered to each other. Izbart had spread the message.

Not all were fans, though. The king raised his hand, and five fingers spread wide, grasping for something out of the empty air. He faced the crowd, and as he breathed in, he puffed up like a cornered house cat, and all went quiet.

"The Spirit of Kivu is the favor we seek," King Ulindi said.

He drove his cane into the silt. "Not reason, not mental magic, not demagoguery."

His eyes shifted, sky-to-ground, person-to-person, and something took up inside him, and he changed as the voluptuous woman could change. His head flapped back onto his nape, making his face flush with the sky. The ritual continued full steam ahead.

Ten thousand eyes fixated on him. Murmurings rose from the rings, expecting something at any moment. The huddled bodies parted, as two men in grimy T-shirts brought forth a leashed goat. They dragged the animal to the center of a human circle and flipped it upside-down. The man at the hind legs smiled with the remnants of three front teeth angled out like a pitchfork. The animal bleated, pulled, curved its form to escape. The three-toothed man slipped a noose around its neck. The king looking up into the sky had cued them as part of the choreography.

The voluptuous woman marched up to the goat. She was there but wasn't there, walking out of her mind to the center of the human circle. The three-toothed man spread the goat's testicles out as a flat sheet of paper. She drew up a short peeler knife near its hind legs. Her eyes pulsed. Oh, no—the knife came down, castrating it. Crimson drops... *drip-drip...drip-drip*, darkened the red dust.

The air felt thinner, as if vacuumed away, making it hard to breathe. With everything happening around us, and the nearly hypnotic state it put everyone in, I didn't know if any plan could work in this place. I wondered if the minds of the men were too far gone. I kept wiping the sweat from my forehead and focused on my breathing.

The long beard of the animal came next. She sliced it off and held up the scraggly blond hairs for confirmation to be given by the ten thousand eyes. A young girl placed a bowl below the upside-down head of the goat. The voluptuous woman unsheathed a long carving knife. I couldn't watch. The knife swooped down and slit the animal's throat. A bag of blood burst open from the flesh, rushed, and pulsed like an unclogged drain pipe into the bowl. I was sickened.

§

The king's head flapped back to see his people. He took them in, one person at a time. The bony fingers spread out over them. "Great power needs energy." He shook his head to find himself. "Our God needs energy. Drink, my God. Drink!" He pointed at the blood. The plateau heard his cry, launching up a second, "Drink, my God!" up into the mist.

The woman looked drained. Her head sunk lower, and white eye paint dripped over her lips. She bowed to the flesh of the animal, to its pink tongue, and the head, which lay whipped around its torso like a wet towel. The woman bowed to the king and finally crashed down on her buttocks.

The king stood over Logos eyeballing him. "Do the Spirit's work for us." His thin arm seemed to lengthen when the bony index finger unfurled toward the stairway. "Go now to attach drill bits." He wasn't asking, either. "Make us strong again," he shouted. The pitch of his voice rose. "Ask our Spirit to help, my son." It floated high and away, castrato, hypnotizing the senses like a young Michael Jackson.

The crowd in the outer ring understood its significance. They looked to the sky, sensing their Spirit arrived in the vessel of the king. What he said next blind-sided us. "Kneel my son. Kneel before me, first."

Logos appeared baffled by the request. Chicotte looked at David, who looked at the king. The button-downs looked at each other.

"With all respect, sir," Logos said. "I won't."

Gasps came from the mass.

§

King Ulindi said Logos needed to kneel, hand over his broken stick, and become like the other Workers. "On your knees. Pride is only the mask of self-esteem. Ask for the Spirit's help."

The rabble silenced and morphed back into an audience, leaving only wind rushing through the acacias.

David heard everything. He removed his hardhat, sighed, and dried his wet forehead on his arm. He wanted to speak.

Logos continued to press. He asked the king, what did this have to do with the drill bit connection?

The king puffed up like a housecat, again. He was an entire foot taller than Logos.

A powwow took place, going something like this: the king wanted Logos to kneel to satisfy his own sense of embarrassment from Logo's comments during their first meeting, and to be publicly acknowledged as the single source of knowledge for his people. He was the oracle; the oracle was him kind of stuff. Two agendas, two audiences, waited for two knees to kneel.

Logos kept his hands at his sides. An abrupt gesture could be misread and end up fatal. He said, quite simply, he wanted to do his job. Could the king try to understand? Let him work freely, let the men work freely, and all Kivu would grow richer than he ever dreamed. He spun it well, but the line between agent provocateur and his own real beliefs blurred. Sometimes, I even heard his father talking about "principles" and all. If Logos was acting, provoking like he told me, damn he was good.

"I understand," the king said. "But it is you who does *not* understand." He stepped away from Logos, ending the powwow. "Kneel, pray to the Spirit," he said aloud.

"I can't pray to your god or any mysticism," Logos replied to everyone.

I wondered how far he'd take this.

The king asked the crowd if they liked what Logos had to say. Who did Logos believe would help him complete this? The king, the Spirit, a god? It couldn't be a simple human like Logos doing it on his own. Only gods glutted nations with food, water, shelter, and wealth.

The crowd inched forward, or sat on the shoulders of other men, or did an endzone run to get closer. Maybe a human sacrifice was to come? Who in the hell knew? I kept on thinking about those creative geniuses in prison planning the breakout, and our Land Rover waiting by.

"What do you believe in?" the king asked.

"Reason"

The king made an old stink face. "This is mind games."

"The mind isn't a game," Logos said. "It's an instrument of progress. Men don't learn by revelation."

It didn't go over too well, and if this were a pot of water, we were two eggs boiling.

A different Logos emerged from all the ones I'd met months ago. The creative dreamer with a dark childhood, the problem-solver who liked to teach, wasn't entirely here anymore. The other one showed. The one with the hard streak. The one who always meant what he said. The one who wouldn't chicken out or buckle under. All the stuff said earlier in the trailer, the "leaving something to last forever" stuff, was about more than sparking a revolt.

"You work for us," the king said. He looked at Logos sideways, like the day in the briefing room. "You work for a Master—me."

The Workers and camos, all ranks, and files, looked down at the red dust.

"I work for myself, only myself," Logos said. "I take satisfaction in the achievement I create." Here stood a man who wouldn't look down.

A purple impatiens floweret flew overhead and landed at the king's feet. The voluptuous woman stared at it, spellbound by its landing. David exchanged a glance with Chicotte, and both took a step forward.

"You play a dangerous game, young man."

32

"I don't want to play this game," Logos said.

He said he should be allowed to complete his work. He should be allowed to make them successful, exactly why they brought him, and without all this pomp. He said they could make something his people could be proud of.

David saw an opening. He came to the king's side. "Sir, let's not forget our goal. We need to complete this, to inaugurate Shaft number four. The money will flow. We'll flood your territory with money. Do you trust me?"

The king nodded and waved the operation forward.

Logos agreed. It's the first time he and David agreed on anything.

"This new drill bit to twister plate connection's never been tried," David whispered to the king. "Let the mechanic get the kinks out. It's why we got him here."

It confirmed everything Logos had told me. The life which crumbled after Chile was true, real, and still exerting a heavy gravity on us. From the day we met, he never lied to me. He'd been hard with his way, and hard with his teachings, and the plan, but never lied about any of it. He'd only gotten into a bad deal and did his best with whatever he had to get us out.

The king extended his bony palm to Logos. "Place the broken stick in my hand, first."

Logos refused.

All the men on the platform looked at each other. They looked at Izbart, and he gave a slight nod back.

King Ulindi thrust two fists over the mass of heads around him. "The Kivu Spirit, Charla, says it must be! The great blackbird which soars above." He looked into the mist for it. "It is our savior, doctor, jester, guardian." The long bony finger curled into a sickle at Logos. "Follow me, my son. Say reason is a lie."

Logos caught sight of me out of the corner of his eye.

"I can't," he said.

"Mechanic, who in the hell are you?"

Man, it sent a shiver through me. Beyond fear of the unknown, a higher threshold waited: the fear of pain. The pain we would suffer if he resisted. His answer made it real.

"I deal with human beings, not spirits," Logos said. "Reason is real. We use it to think, to make decisions with, and I'll defend it with my life."

Holy crap.

The king weighed it for truth. "You would die for this, this principle?"

Logos looked at the king and at Eden. "Yes."

There was no turning back now, for any of us.

Howls flew over the plateau, cheering Logos. Flowerets landed all around. The mass broke up, moving and shifting toward our group near the headframe. The blue camos surrounding the king pushed them back, and some fell on the ground. The old and feeble and too young to stand on their own were crushed. The adults and the strong didn't like it, and thrust their fists in the air, and devolved back into a mob.

The king sighted his cane like a handgun at everyone. He made it clear: the KEM collective ran the mine. His decision made their decision, so enough with these games.

Voices shouted at him to let Logos continue. A T-shirted man broke through a ring, bumped into the King. The nerve. Two blue camos dragged the man away by his feet and more blue camos came around the king. Our new grand scheme wasn't going according to plan.

§

David removed his hardhat and bowed to the king like any old nobleman seen in a history textbook. "King Ulindi, an idea." He shifted a quarter to Logos. "Your freedom, Logos. You got it, immediately after the successful connection. The rest of the money in your account, too. It's a promise." He nodded to the king.

Logos didn't wag his tail with the gratitude of a stray or anything. He took his time. He demanded David say it louder, for all to hear. He wanted it loud and clear, for even those in the outer ring to hear.

David repeated it, loud and clear.

"You'll release us after," Logos said. "You'll pay us and each man here like independent traders."

David stayed quiet for too long. "*Yes*."

Chicotte agreed. It didn't take too long, as he eyed the top of the headframe. He knew it was as close to a temple as a man could have in this time, and only one man could make it into something real for its followers.

When the Masters agreed with Logos, the Workers and camos and half-men stragglers all looked at each other. People stood with mouths agape, or whispered, and some hugged complete strangers.

A calm came over Logos. He stood with his arms hanging down, one over the other. The right palm clasped the back of the other over his waist. A rank of hardhats behind us clasped their hands over the same way. The T-shirts behind them followed.

King Ulindi pointed at the zigzagging stairs, which seemed to rise into the heavens. The stairs weren't floating in the clouds, or didn't become a mystical trunk like in *Jack and the Beanstalk*, or anything dramatic the way I mentioned it. The expectation of the final job, and everything we had gone through to get to this point, made it a daunting climb. For the others who worked atop the structure every day, it became routine. You see things relative to where you came from, and where you come to stand. Each person takes their own road, has their own perception, I guess, but everyone standing around us, who had worked at Logos's side, looked up. Our future waited for us up there.

33
THE CLIMB

The mist fell behind the stairs, over the mountain ridge, scattering over the platform like a dust. At the top of the ridge, it flowed down in a solid column, disguising the foliage, a mask as much as a monolith. Where it became a solid, the monolith said nothing, gave up nothing, and made you work to understand it. If I didn't focus, it made my thinking fuzzy again.

A ramp led to a rickety metal balustrade one-inch around. It rattled, and swayed, as if the whole damned thing could come crumbling down at any moment. These cheap bastards had recycled the old A-frame stairway to save money, and probably attached it with chewing gum. Below the rails, no side panel protected the body. If a climber didn't hold tight when up high, he could fall through the opening, way, way down there. My good right arm held tight doing the work for two.

We climbed. A blue camo led the way up, followed by a brown camo, Logos, me, another brown camo, a blue camo behind him, a line of hardhats, and T-shirted men. The camos' Uncle Kalashnikovs flapped over their shoulders. No turning back now.

One foot went in front of the other. One of my knees went high, while the other disappeared, over, and over. The old knees knocked and told me the truth. If we didn't hit the mark on the plan, we might be thrown off the platform, or worse, made permanent subjects of the Masters out in the snake and rodent wing.

In the moment, I no longer had a past. No future waited. I lived in the narrow present, to step, step, step. Men pressed up the stairway behind us in line; Worker-men, armed men, all men, climbing up to pray, or proselytize before the temple. My heart pounded—*thump, thump,* again, *thump, thump.* Up near forty feet, the steel-girded top came into view. I could hear, smell, touch but not see up clearly; my head angled down to my feet for sure stepping. The line grew impatient, and each step up produced a thud which shook the entire ladder and returned as a shockwave.

At the top, the nothingness outside the fence came into view, the crowd, the plateau, the giant open-pit, black-green treetops to the horizon, and zephyrs carrying the white mist over the sunshine. The tower of the radio room-prison plucked its head over the trees in the distance. Somewhere out there, the Land Rover was waiting to take us there. Logos would make an opening in the fence, and we would drive away, happy, and relieved, and hidden behind the falling mist...

Logos extended his hand out to Izbart and Jando and they each shook it.

Izbart tapped his heart. He placed his hand on Logos's shoulder. "Good to see you, sir."

"Good to see you both," he said. Logos wanted to say more, but too many of the king's guards stood around like noisy mothers-in-law.

§

In the middle of the floor, a crashed flying saucer leaned to its side. This was the infamous twister plate, which sent other mechanics missing, and caused the village's pain. It was a concave dish, six feet in diameter, with deep threaded holes, and looked like Logos's drawings. When prepped, the drill bits attached to the plate, and the plate to the drill rod.

My book described it differently, but this job screamed custom all the way.

They led him to it. The plate had been brought up earlier by pulleys, as before, when I got injured by the you-know-who son-of-a-bitch bastard prick. Logos planned this install out better than before. To ensure no dust, or man-made obstructions made their way into the threaded holes, the attaching would be done up on the platform. Once coupled, the pair would be returned to the ground level by a crane for the final attachment to the drill rod itself. Logos took no chances.

I heard more boots on the stairway. Marc and Chicotte hurried up as if evacuating a fire, only going the wrong way. They stood atop the platform. Mr. K. K. came up behind them. Marc took in the view and waddled about all cocksure, like we were playing in his backyard, and he was providing the toys.

Chicotte examined the twister plate. The scent of whiskey blew in his wake, and even the hardhats exchanged glances with the T-shirts. He bent down to the bored holes of the plate, looking into their depths, red flares over his eyes.

Logos studied the drill rod. It hung down forty feet within the bowels of the A-frame. The wind kicked up, sending it skidding up against the black steel. This produced a dinging sound, drowning out whatever conversation hung in the air. Our feet up to our knees shuddered each time.

The twister plate rolled. I helped Izbart and Jando steady it. My bad arm held me back from the heavy stuff, but I would do my part. After a while, I even forgot the occasional shooting pains.

Logos withdrew what looked like a thin periodontal probe from his jumpsuit pocket. He inserted it through and over each thread in the screw holes. This ensured the thread of each hole ran clean, ready for the tight fitting of the drill bits. He inserted a round mirror into the hole like a dental exam.

"Any cavities or critters?" I said.

He shook his head.

"How's the spark coming?"

"It's coming."

Well, where was the rest of it? Improvising as he went along? For god's sake, let me know what you're going to do before you do it. "Give me a signal, I'm shitting."

He went back to work.

Izbart waved at the hardhats to begin. Two of them pulled an immense drill bit in the back of a cart. The head connected into a six-foot-long shaft which resembled an artillery gun projecting from a tank. This was one of the critters we had transported in the crates. The mammoth tri-cone head held diamond inserts, the man-made, industrial-types promoted as stronger than any other substance and looked like scallops on a riddled face. Diamonds cutting for diamonds, only a "beginner" like me could see the irony.

Izbart studied it. "I never see this kind before," he said. "Yes, will take a great man to fix." He glanced at Logos.

"Made for him," Chicotte said, slurring at times. "F...for this site only."

Marc came over, knelt, and patted the bit on the head. "Igneous rock requires the hardest substance to penetrate." He looked down to ground level, in David's direction. "Paid for by the Consortium." He raised his forefinger at Jando. "Don't mess it up."

"Yes sir," Jando said.

Marc told Logos not to mess it up. He tapped his temple to remember the mechanic who went bye-bye.

"Mr. Logos will not mess it up," Jando said.

Mr. K. K. stood by the edge of the platform looking out into the void. At times, he watched the action, but never looked my way.

§

The rest of us got to work. The sky darkened, and the air cooled, and the front from last night, the harbinger. A cloud burst.

Marc ambled about, looking for something. "The rain," he yelled to everyone.

A wall of rain pushed in from over the mountain top. Half of the dozen men on the platform looked, the others continued securing harnesses, pulling cables, tightening vices.

Marc noticed. He insisted, "Look, rain!"

Every man took in the wall of water.

I stood behind all the men and could see Marc in my periphery. He took rabbit steps to the twister plate and knelt next to it. He coughed, raised his fist to his mouth, brought it back down, unclenched it over the large center hole of the twister plate. His palm remained there, flat and firm over the hole. When he looked back at me, my head stayed still. He didn't see me see him.

34

They sent me down the stairway to help secure the shifting drill rod. There were other workers available, but Marc spoke with Izbart about me, specifically. I tried to signal Logos but missed him when I descended the stairs.

While on the ground, the gale built-up and carved through the green, pushing men, and light equipment aside like confetti. We were soaked to the bone. It took six of us to steady the drill rod with reinforced straps. I used one arm and all my weight. When it wasn't enough, the caveman club helped too. I didn't feel the pain anymore. I came back up.

§

Izbart, Jando, and two hardhats held the plate steady as Logos connected the mammoth bit into the center hole. Rain beaded on his face; his black jumpsuit stuck. The bit wouldn't take. He remained steady, went down the line of risk, odds, and good old common sense in his head. I caught eyes with him, shifting my gaze toward Marc. Logos got it—he always got it.

He ordered the drill bit removed from the plate. Logos instructed Jando to probe for obstructions in the center hole. His hand came out holding what looked like a tiny, rusted doughnut. He brought it to Logos.

Logos held it up for all to see. "An old ball bearing," he said to everyone. "This has no business there."

Izbart examined it. "I agree."

Logos fixed his gaze on Marc.

"Don't look at me," Marc said.

Chicotte came over. "You." He waited for a reply, even a squeal, but none came. Chicotte ignited. "How this happen? *Tell me*." He wasn't entirely sure about Marc and studied the faces of the men lined up. He stumbled once or twice.

Marc pointed to the rest of us on the platform as culprits.

The rain eased up, but the wind stayed, pushing by the plateau.

§

Chicotte looked into each man and could sense the slightest nerve or increased pulse, equipped like some human lie detector. Everyone looked straight ahead. He returned to Marc. He didn't buy this Englishman's wild goose chase.

"I say, why on earth are you looking at me?" Marc said. He breathed harder. "My god."

Chicotte's index finger rose to Marc's nose. "I deal with you later," he whispered.

Marc's head tilted back to avoid the thick fingernail scraping his septum. A smash and grab—Chicotte swiped the gold spectacles from Marc's face. They disappeared into Chicotte's pants pocket.

"Drunken wanker! Need those. Return them to me, at once." Marc lost his balance.

I have seen people I know without their glasses before. Most would say, they usually looked younger, more vibrant. Marc didn't. He looked like a man ten years past his age, twenty years past his prime. Without his gold specs, his body languished too. He clung to the steel girding, protecting his thin torso from the gusts.

Logos examined the threads of the bits for damage. He wasn't sure but said, "Let's go."

"Yes, sir," Izbart said. "Jando, come."

Jando, and a half dozen others, moved to attach the mammoth blue bit to the plate. It weighed like hell, and the strain on the men's faces showed it. They sweat, their muscles pulsed, and they left behind a bit of themselves with each heave, throw, and yank.

Logos pushed the drill bit and twister plate closer. He stepped back. "There's a small gap, still." He called Izbart and the others over.

Izbart could tell. "The tooling no good," Izbart said. "Fabrication problem, yes?" He looked at Logos.

Logos nodded; it won't take.

Oh, man, this needed to work. Any spark would only come from the men seeing him achieve what the king said was impossible without him, and the divine, and all. If one mortal could do it, so could another. If it didn't work, the spark and revolt might bite us on the ass.

The mob below whispered, whistled, booed, and howled. Whoosh—the ruckus soared over the platform, over our heads like a burst of air.

King Ulindi faced the crowd. He raised his arms and they quieted. As his right shoulder fell, the voluptuous woman caressed it.

Chicotte paced about the platform, sharp looks aimed at the faces of the men. He arrived at the place he feared. There were no more people to kidnap, or beat over the head, or extort. Only one man remained to shoulder this to its completion. The man he'd dealt with across the foldout table for the past six months.

"Do something, my friend," Chicotte said to Logos, "or else." He looked at me as much as Logos.

My knees shook. I went over to Logos. "You're going to get us killed." I had enough and pressed him for an answer. "You making all this up?" I never forgot what he said to me.

"I've been planning this since day one." He was serious as all hell, too. "Whenever you saw me quiet as a mouse, I was thinking about it. Whenever I busted my hands on the generators and dinosaurs and all their other crap, I was thinking about it. Whenever they tried to fuck us, I was thinking about it. You got me? When they closed the gate behind us for the first time, I said to myself, they better watch out."

He knew about the paperback and prison break and those genius guys planning it out from the start. I saw it now. He knew the warden, guards, and iron fist institution had a million things to consider preventing an escape, but the jailbirds only had *one* thing to consider—escape. It was their advantage. It was right under their nose and ours. It was our advantage, too, and he played the nothing to lose card right up to the edge of the platform.

§

King Ulindi and his court stared at us from below. The voluptuous woman whispered something to him. The last thing I expected is what she did. She shot one of those wicked glances of hers. The look tried to catch you and impale your mind. It impaled the weak. It impaled the ignorant. It impaled the untrained irrational mind. It controlled the minds who'd been robbed of their self-esteem. I knew Logos would see it coming, dodge its barb, and laugh it off. She smiled something crooked my way, but I could handle it now. I'd seen this kind of mumbo jumbo mind game before.

Logos blew it off. He paced in front of the twister plate, searching for the solution to close the gap. The ten thousand eyes were on him, including Eden's. He stopped, put his thumb to his bottom lip, talked to himself. An eternal forty minutes past. The impatience for action grew, but he acted on his own clock.

§

Feet thumped the stairs. The king, with the voluptuous woman in tow, came up onto the platform. He looked every man in the face, and the men looked down at the steel floor.

The king stepped back near the edge. He looked on with Chicotte and the voluptuous woman, hoping their expectation exacted a weight on Logos. The three cozied up a degree as if watching a ball game from their box seats. They relaxed their postures without ever relaxing their expectation on the man in front of them.

Logos paced. I imagined he went to the place which gave him refuge from all this. The place where the silver cord lifted the good ones up and away, and they could look down seeing it all better than anyone because they saw everything before; and the good could either figure a way out or forget what came before. He wouldn't forget, and the tinder may come, now more than ever, for the grand scheme to burn baby burn.

§

After more than three hours, the narrow plane five stories in the air became the only world I knew. Everything else fell off the edge of the platform, including my past and future. Only the objective now existed, as the light of day slipped away. It *can* happen that fast.

Logos opened his rucksack and removed the clock. I didn't know what in the hell this had to do with the new grand scheme, but I figured he did. He studied the large gear which remained, eyes down, head down, lost. He ripped it free.

35

No one knew what he planned to do with it. No signal came from him, no heads-up, or thumbs down about our chances. He did what he did, knowing he was right, and you had to watch.

Jando and the others pulled out the drill bit again. Logos slipped the gear over the thin rod jutting out behind the drill rod. It fit. I could see his thinking: use the clock gear as a giant washer, or filler, closing the gap made by the error in the factory tooling. It might work. He placed the ball bearing shipped from South Africa over it.

Marc squinted at the simple fix. "Ha, ha. You can't be serious? This is for professionals, not shady tree mechanics."

Logos looked for something more to finish the job. He withdrew a hulking piece of steel from under the operator's control. It was a pipe wrench found in any drawer or beneath Mom's sink but on steroids. Taller than him, the wrench's weight told him when and how to walk when he shouldered it over the wet floor.

Jando and Izbart tried to help, but Logos walked through them.

Rain again, soft, and light, and misty-white.

He turned the worm screw, adjusting the jaw of the wrench to wrap around the base of the drill bit. He stood over the plate, pushed the wrench with all his body behind him. Nothing moved or clicked the way it should. He bent down, hands on knees to catch his breath. His jumpsuit glistened from the sweat rolling up beneath it, and rain tapping its surface. He stood over the plate again, pulled the wrench with finesse and brute force—all at once—every muscle shaking. He fell over the wrench and crashed on the platform. It was the only time I ever saw him flat on the ground; the only time he ever looked up at me unsure.

Izbart ran to him. He shot a glance at the conjoined parts. He couldn't speak. "The fitting is tight," Izbart said to himself. He turned to those in the box seats. "The fitting is tight." He ran to the edge of the platform, raindrops streaking across his jaw. *"The fitting is tight!"* He jumped up and down. He looked back at Logos, who sat slumped down over his knees on the wet steel. Izbart tried to help him up and I followed. "You have done it, sir," he said. "Will work now. I send Jando down to make sure."

Jando and the hardhats guided the crane, as it moved the connected plate down to ground level.

Logos caught his breath, letting it all sink in. In between the huffs and puffs, he glanced at Izbart, me, and the Workers.

For some reason, I couldn't recognize the Logos I knew, as his whole being seemed removed from the platform. I extended my hand to him. He held it tight, shook it, and I knew he'd be all right.

Jando returned. He stayed quiet for too long and bit his lip the same goddamn way when he told me about my arm.

"Success, sir," he said, choked up. "It run."

Chicotte clapped, prompting the rest of the court to clap as well. He stood near Logos, facing the crowd. The stage belonged to Chicotte. His arms spread wide, palms forward, raindrops beading on the back of his thick pope-hands. "It is done. We. Live. Again!"

The crowd blew up from there. Thousands jumped, danced, embraced each other, and even rolled on the ground. Pink and yellow flowers flew about, and the purple impatiens, too. Hugs, handshakes, and jumps for joy shook the platform. The men working congratulated one another, and shook Logos's hand, or touched him.

Logos dented a smile from the side of his mouth. He was drained, sitting on the floor, arms wrapped around his bent knees, breathing and breathing.

The two hardhats, which pulled the bit in the cart, came over, and lifted Logos onto their shoulders. Everyone else followed in a line behind them. They carried him to the edge of the platform for all to see. The men carrying him hollered:

Ji-jo, ji-jo, ji-jo.

All the men joined in and hopped up and down.

Ji-jo, ji-jo, ji-jo.

Thousands of arms extended out from the crowd below, seeking to touch Logos. The men placed him back down near the edge.

Eden took a step closer to the foot of the stairway, and their eyes met, and if they could only reach out and embrace each other, their bodies might float up together again, up and away, to the place, or cloud where the sun shined silver and warmed with quiet.

He caught his breath and turned to me. I can tell you now, I was never as proud of another man as on that day. He stated what he would do from the beginning, planned it, fought Hell for it, and did it. I only helped. He made history. La Petite Ville, and the whole goddamned region, would never be the same.

"Why doesn't the mouse run from the elephant?" he said to me. "Because he's no longer afraid."

To control the fear, control the mind. I thought. It became clear. I was coming closer to understanding my inner demon.

Logos turned back to face the crowd.

The king approached, clapping a fake aristocrat clap; the one where the palms never actually touch. He motioned for four blue camos, with Mr. K. K. in the lead, to come alongside Logos.

The king's fingers cut over the crowd. "Tell the good people *my* Spirit did this for you," he said for all to hear. "Say, I allowed you to achieve this."

Logos looked at me. "No. A man with a mind achieved it."

My insides ripped apart knowing what may come.

The king nodded for the guards to tighten around Logos.

It didn't make any sense. How could something go from the achievement of a lifetime and history written, to a bag of wet nothing and worse ever? Where were the Workers in all this? Why didn't they come running to his side?

I ran to him.

"Robert, don't," Logos said.

Mr. K. K. came next to me. His head turned. The pupils magnified. The yolks shimmered and drew me closer. In my mind, I fell inside. I saw directly into the eyes of the blackbird for the first time. I saw the infinite and the cold and the nothing. I struggled to breathe, to control the fear. I stood before a silver-framed mirror in the space. My eyes dilated, jaw crept open, teeth showing, ready to strike. It was happening again. Mr. K. K. looked back at me in the mirror. He was the size of a child but old and shivering, and we were the same. He covered himself, fearful the prophet Charla might smack down on him like thunder or rain. The feral look in his eye wasn't real, simply a mask for a mind which couldn't control things—an irrational mind.

Hate was the consequence of fear. VMA preached it, only I never heard. It takes a while, a lifetime even, but eventually we listen. In here, I saw things for what they were, and the ticking in me fell away. *Fear is in the mind. The mind must control the fear.* I felt calm and control. I came out of the space—out of the old noggin of mine.

The men on the platform stood as before. No time had elapsed, and no jump cut in the film, like before when I got injured. Mr. K. K.'s boots scraped the edge. I could have pushed him from the platform, made it look like a T-shirt bumped into him—oops. I resisted.

The waterfall no longer rushed in me. The fuzziness, blinding white, all gone for good. I was in control, but a different version of myself; I no longer feared. I held the reins of reason for the first time.

36
THE LAST CHAPTER

The king faced the mist over the ridge. He was half-man, half-Spirit again, when his long thin finger pointed at Logos. "What power made this miracle?" he said.

Logos clasped his right hand over the back of the left. The arms hung down at five-thirty, legs apart, balanced on the edge of the platform.

"I told you already," Logos said. "Reason."

"Death to you!"

I thought I misheard. I didn't. The crowd heard it correctly. The words struck them as a blast wave, leaving shock and silence. Their faces were wiped clear of features, as if the blast could erase noses, eyes, eyebrows, and lips. A ruin of blank heads and torsos remained, frozen in the ash of time like Pompeii. David vanished.

A cry from the ground. "No. Logos, please," Eden said.

Her pleas echoed and fell away in the rush of air going through the acacias.

The Workers all stood behind Logos, pushed there by the blue camos. Each hardhat clasped his hands over the same way. The T-shirts made to stand behind the hardhats, did the same with their hands. Over the edge below, Workers of all ranks clasped their hands the same way.

Eden noticed them. She took the hand of a little pigtailed girl. The girl's other arm sat in a sling and cast. Some of the children near the girl mimicked the hands of the men.

"Who is the God?" the king said. He came close to Logos. "Say your reason is a lie." As serious as any man in front of another, the king asked him why he wouldn't recant.

"What is the difference between a thing and a principle?" Logos said. "A thing dies, a principle lives on."

This was no act, no agent provocateur stuff. He believed it, would die for it, and we stood as witnesses. A shudder went through me.

The king waved to Chicotte, who grabbed Logos around the neck, and choked him in a half nelson.

"*Logos*," Eden cried out.

Two blue camos held me back.

Logos twisted away and threw an uppercut, popping Chicotte's head back. The big man struck him with an elbow to the temple. Logos fell and didn't move. Chicotte smothered him. It went silent.

§

Blue camos pulled the bodies out. Logos lay there. The one side of his face sunk hard into the damp platform. Chicotte got up.

I waited for a sign he was all right, but his chest didn't move up or down like mine or yours did, anymore, and his stillness didn't twitch or shift. Guards moved toward him and dragged him away.

"*Stop*," I said.

Eden reached up with one arm. "My King, please."

Her voice came up, echoed off the steel, and drifted over the edge like a feather. The king looked down, seeing Eden distraught and falling apart. Her eyes had shrunken into reddish pinwheels from the tears. King Ulindi noticed the pigtailed girl. She saw Eden wailing and clutched Eden's leg.

"Matilde," the king called out.

Matilde looked up at her father.

He returned a numb stare at the little girl. The camos dragged Logos away over the wet platform.

"Stop," King Ulindi said to the guards. "Enough."

The guards stepped away from Logos but kept a tight knot around him.

I didn't know what to do.

Izbart waved for the Workers to come over, and they made two ranks, as a passageway leading me off the platform, to the ground. Izbart and Jando stood nearest me, at the opening. Izbart put his hand on my shoulder and shook his head at me. The corners of his eyes had turned fleshy. He said my job was finished, and they would handle it from here. He held his chin up the whole time.

Jando bit his lip. When his hat fell over his eyes, I pushed it back up.

Metal drummed metal. The blue and brown placed their Kalashnikovs flat on the platform. The guards on the ground did the same thing. Everyone looked at them. All the Master guards clasped their right hands over the back of their lefts, over their belts.

Logos groaned. He flipped over and stared at me through one mashed cherry eye. He was alive—thank god.

My eyes told Jando and another hardhat to grab him. They carried him off the platform. When they reached the bottom of the stairway, Eden rushed him to one of the vans. The people parted for them to pass, and the van faded into the multitude.

I stood alone. I looked to the floor for something, I didn't know what. Tears filled my eyes. The old chasm opened inside of me for more tears to rush in but I said no. I dammed them back. I could control the chasm now, to open, or close it at will.

Marc sat several yards away, blinded in vertigo, and squeezing his temples. He called out to me; I didn't answer.

The crowd rushed at the platform. Leading the T-shirts, frocks, and gunnysack ponchos, the businessmen in their button-downs. A dozen of them ran toward the platform, with camos protecting them. Rain continued to patter, and their shirts stuck to their backs like those old artisan miners who panned in the muck. They thrust their fists and yelled at the king, Chicotte, and the voluptuous woman. The camos even pointed and screamed at the king's group; so many people, so many bodies, all crashing towards us.

A pair of the king's blue camos still held their uncles and came at me.

Izbart's eyes told me run—now—run as fast as I could. Take the passageway—go.

I saw the stairs, but instead, I stepped forward. I stood at the edge of the platform. My eyes teared, but I held it all back. The Workers stood on either side of me. Izbart stood next to me. I clasped the back of my left palm with my right. I stood upright and solid. A breeze brushed my face, cooling it on one side. The drizzle slowed, and clouds moved away, peeling back a wide pink-orange sky. Over the ridge, I could see through the mist for the first time, through the nothingness.

Readers Guide: Questions and Topics for Discussion

1. Before reading *Feral Eye of the Blackbird*, how much did you know about Africa, forced labor, mining, and collectivism?

2. Why do you think Robert Bonhomme and Logos were drawn into the trip without all the details known beforehand?

3. How does this story bring to light the ideological clash between collectivism, capitalism, and the rise of socialism in Western democracies? Did you learn anything about this period in history?

4. Why did Logos agree to take Robert as his assistant on the trip? Are they real friends? Can you imagine ever doing what Robert or Logos did?

5. What is Robert's most admirable quality? What is Logos's? What is each man's least admirable quality? Are they people you would want to have known?

6. Mr. K. K., Chicotte, Marc, Eden and Izbart are all important characters in this book. Who will you remember most and why?

7. Why did Logos fall for Eden? Why did she fall for him? Are there similarities between their life decisions and yours? Is she a realistic character?

8. What did you think of the hierarchy in place at the mine? What role did racism play?

9. What will you remember most about this book? Is there a favorite scene in *Feral Eye of the Blackbird*? Do you plan to read more about this time in history?

10. Do you think Logos's strong personality helped or hurt them? Could they have escaped another way?

11. What were your impressions of the author's voice and style? What specific themes did John Katsoulis emphasize throughout the book?

12. What did you like or dislike about the book which hasn't been discussed already?

13. What is your favorite line?

14. If this book were to be made into a movie, whom would you cast for the main roles?